For Pat —
   The Wednesday Queen
+ other days too —
      With love

Aug
2016

GRAB BAG YEARS

1939-1941

Emily Boone Ruch

by
EMILY BOONE RUCH

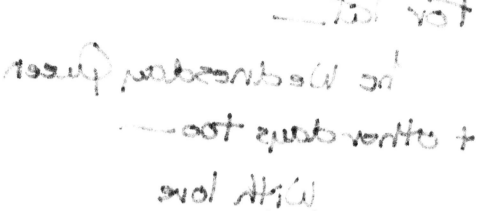

First American Edition

David Yawn, Editor

Corporate Chronicles

A Lighthouse Leadership Imprint

David Yawn Communications

1082 Kings Park Road

Memphis, TN 38117

Designed by Gloria C. White & Associates, Memphis, TN

Chapter I

THE TRAIN RIDE: FIRST DAY

Momma and Poppa take us to the train station. "Do you have plenty of money for tipping?" Poppa looks anxiously at Gamma. "You know it's ten cents a bag. And give the porter 50 cents for each berth he makes up." Poppa reaches inside his suit coat pocket to pull out his wallet.

Momma looks up at him and stops him. "They have enough. Mama and I have figured this carefully. Haven't we, Mama?"

Gamma nods, bites her lip and clasps her big practical black handbag to herself. She looks really nice in her new dark green shirtwaist. Green is her favorite color because, she says, God made so much of it.

Poppa takes the pocket watch from his vest pocket and peers through his wire-rimmed bifocals. "It's almost 9:15. Trains run on time, you know."

"Board. Board ... All aboard."

"Here, Tootsie," he says to me, his dark blue eyes twinkling, "You're off on an adventure — to the Rhode Island seashore — and to celebrate your tenth birthday! Charm those Yankees, you hear. And be sure your grandmother stays out of trouble." He bends down and hugs me hard.

1

"Your first summer away," Momma sighs, her warm brown eyes full of tears. "Remember to write. Now," Momma scans in front of her and behind her, "Where is your brother Bill? He was here a minute ago." Her left eyebrow goes up and she twirls around in the direction of the station, her brown and white spectators making time on the station platform.

"Come, Gamma. Trains don't wait. You and Eliza get on. Up you go." Poppa gives us each a lift up the big yellow step stool. He peers in the direction of the station and mutters half aloud, "It'll serve him right if he misses the train."

"'Board ... 'board." The train begins to move.

"Bye, Momma. Bye, Poppa. Oh! Here comes Bill!"

Bill races up, his white shirt tail flying, his new size 12 tennis shoes looking like a clown's; and he makes a long-legged leap into the open train door. _Flash Gordon_ and _Dick Tracy_ are tucked under one arm; he tosses me _Little Orphan Annie_. "I made it!" he shouts.

Gamma, Momma and I cheer.

But Poppa shakes his head and growls, "Stupid smart aleck."

I glance at Bill. His triumphant face has gone pinched.

"Poppa didn't mean what he said, Bill." I put my hand on his arm. "I think he meant that you might have missed the train ... or ... broken your neck."

Bill shrugs his shoulders.

Gamma directs us to a pair of green wool double seats that face each other and have a big window in between. "I choose the middle of the car because it is rough riding at the ends over the wheels. And I always sit _with_ the direction of the train. It makes me seasick to ride backward."

"Nothing makes me seasick," counters Bill as he charges off in his #12's to explore. The train lunges and lurches until we get out of

Memphis[1] and then it settles down to a steady rocking which makes me sleepy. I lean my head against the window pane and watch the telephone poles glide by through half-opened eyes.

Why does Poppa have to yell at Bill? It makes my stomach hurt.

After a while, Gamma opens her black bag and pulls out our picnic lunch of ham, pickle, and mustard sandwiches on rye bread and peanut butter and jelly sandwiches on soft white bread and hard boiled eggs, and we buy cold cokes from the man going through the cars. "We'll eat dinner in the diner," she promises as she pushes a hairpin back into her bun.

"Your hair looks nice, Gamma." I notice it's wavier.

"Thank you, Eliza. It's a three-hour hot chore to get a permanent wave." She proudly pats her gray and white waves.

I read all the comic books and color in a new Princess Elizabeth and Margaret Rose coloring book, and then lie down on the itchy green seats and take a snooze. When I awaken, the world outside is a different color.

"Wash your hands for dinner," and we weave our way to the lavatory. It is paneled in shiny brown wood and has small built-in sinks and soap in little squirt containers on the wall and ironed white towels that say *Pullman* on them in blue. Bill leads as we weave and jerk our way through the doors leading to and from each car. When we open the out door, the noise is loud and we hold onto each other to sort of jump and pull open the next heavy door.

"The smokestack soot gets in your eyes and all over you," I say. "Gamma, I'm glad you told me to wear a dark dress." I like my navy blue dress anyway. It matches my navy blue eyes and it goes in at the waist and has pleats all around. Maybe the soot will wipe off

---

[1] *L and N Railroad (Louisville & Nashville) had a route from Memphis to New York City.*

my white sandals. If not, I can polish them. Gamma didn't wear her summer shoes.

The diner is near the end of the train, so we pass through other green Pullman cars and some grey ones that are coach cars and don't make up into berths at night.

"Do these people sit up all night?" I ask.

"Some do, but some may get off before night."

"Oh. But why would anyone want to sit up all night?"

"They want to warn the engineer if the bridge ahead is out," replies Bill.

"Oh, Bill."

He laughs and gives one of my brown ponytails a pull.

"The coach cars are cheaper[2]," Gamma explains, "and some folks say they can't sleep on a train anyway. So they might as well save the fare." We tilt our way through a car that has no seats, just a small aisle and many closed doors. "Compartments. The most expensive way to travel," Gamma sniffs.

"I smell cooking!" The diner is silver and white and with lots of tables with white table cloths and a silver vase holding a pink carnation. I peep inside the kitchen. It is tiny and shiny.

"Don't order soup," warns Bill.

"Why not?"

"It's pizened."

"Aw, Bill. Gamma, is it true?"

"Of course not. I think your brother is warning you that soup might slosh all over you when the train goes around a sharp curve or stops suddenly. Are you going to choose your usual favorite, fried chicken?"

---

[2] *Round trip fares from Memphis to NYC*
Coach fare: 34.30, Pullman fare: 58.98 plus Pullman space

"Yes, fried chicken and rice and gravy and rolls and green peas, please." A smiling waiter in a starched white coat takes our order, and I ask him if the cook can do all that in the tiny kitchen.

"Sho' can, Missie. Ain't you havin' onion soup?"

"Oh, no, thank you. I never eat soup on the train."

The dinner is wonderful. Using little silver salt and pepper shakers and big stiff white napkins, watching the stars come and having ice-cream in little silver dishes, and all the time rocking through the night ... I can't believe it!

We lurch our way back with more ease and pass a sign

```
DINING CAR
OTHER
DIRECTION
```

Bill turns it over without even a pause in his step.

```
DINING CAR
THIS WAY
```

He grins at me and winks.

Our porter, Lincoln, has made our seats into a berth for Gamma. He has pulled down the bin from overhead and made a berth for me and another one for Bill. Our whole car is a dark green passageway! Mysterious and so quiet I want to whisper. Lincoln shows me how to climb the ladder and I crawl through the heavy dark green wool curtains to my beautiful, snowy white, snugly bed. My shoes and clothes I put in the little net hammock and change into my seer-sucker pajamas. I am too excited to sleep.

Gamma's round, bespectacled face peeps through my curtains, "Button your curtains from the inside, but if you need anything, just call; Bill or I will hear you. Or push that little button and Lincoln will come. When we wake up in the morning, we'll be in Grand Central Station in New York City!"

My heart is beating so fast. Clickety-clack, clickety-clack, clickety-clack ... whoo ... whoo ... clickety-clack ... whoo ... whoo.

Chapter II

ARRIVING IN PROVIDENCE
AND ON TO MALLOW MARVEL FARM

It is still dark when I open my eyes, but something is different. We aren't moving! I don't have a window in my upper berth, so I dress quickly, unbutton my curtain and jump down. Some berths are already returned to the daytime look and I can see out of those windows. We are in the station in New York City!

"Gamma, where do we look for our train to Providence? There are so many."

"Read the signs, silly," says Bill, as we scurry through the dim light of the station.

"Well, silly, how do we know someone has not changed them? The way you did the dining car sign?"

We do find the right train and hear the call, "'Board ... 'Board. All a-board" and hop on like old hands. In the afternoon, we arrive in Providence and Uncle Henry greets us, with his pipe in his hand.

"Glad to see you, Sister," he hugs Gamma. A handshake for Bill. "Welcome back, Bill. A foot taller?" he smiles.

"Almost 14, Sir," answers Bill proudly.

And then he stoops and levels his blue, blue eyes at mine. "Welcome, Eliza."

We drive the 37 miles to the farm. Instead of horses and cotton,

I see cows and chickens with reddish feathers and a red comb.

"Those are Rhode Island Reds," explains Gamma. Suddenly, the air has a different smell. It is fresh and wonderful. It is the sea smell. We catch glimpses of the sea, so blue, so blue. As blue as Uncle Henry's eyes. Then we drive through a small village with a white wooden church with a steeple and a grocery store and a fire station and a few shops. The Commons, it is called: the center of Little Compton.

"Welcome to Mallow Marvel Farm," announces Uncle Henry as he removes his hat and runs his slender tanned fingers through his thin white hair.

A two-story white clapboard house with a rock fence in the front, covered over with flowers, all rosy pink!

"Mallows," says Gamma as she lightly touches the beautiful pink flowers. "And they are marvels," she adds, "because they bloom exactly the time Uncle Henry and his family are at the farm, from June the first to September. And if you crush the green leaves, you will get a mallow musky smell."

I can picture Gamma making her spicy potpourri, but Bill, who visited the summer before, is out of the car and gone. He comes back in a few minutes. "It's still there, Uncle Henry."

"What is, Bill?"

"The sign in the tool shed. You didn't take it down."

> ## BILL, A PLACE FOR EVERYTHING
> ## AND EVERYTHING IN ITS PLACE

Uncle Henry smiles. "Must be there for some reason."

Bill smiles back. "Come on, Eliza, I'll show you the apple orchard."

We run behind the white farm house and the stone tool shed and the weathered, shingled corn crib, where Bill will stay, and creek open the dark green gate that leads to the apple orchard. I can smell apples. I can't believe my nose. I can smell sea and apples and the sun is beating down warm but not hot. Not like Memphis-hot.

"Look, Bill, here is a dead tree and one that looks half-dead."

"Hurricane damage," nods Bill knowingly. "Last year, 1938, there was a terrible hurricane that tore up trees by their roots and ripped shingles off the roofs. Salt water spray was blown up as far as the orchard! That's what killed these trees. Winds were clocked at 100 miles an hour!"

"Honest true? Are you sure you're not just making that up?"

"It's true. You can't tell the difference between teasing and truth?"

I don't guess I can. I'll have to think about that. We run past the flower garden ... pink roses and white roses and white daisies with yellow centers and some flowers I don't know, but Gamma will for sure. Next the vegetable garden. Tomatoes, carrots, and green beans ... and then we slow down and ease through scratchy brambles on a sort of path.

"Oh, Bill, there's the ocean!" I see just beyond the tall tan grasses ... sand and more sand and the blue, blue sea as wide as I can see to the left and to the right. Crash-sounds as the waves hit the sand hard and turn into white foam. I have never seen the ocean. "It's so big and it smells good! I love it!"

"Eliza ... EEE ... liii ... za!" A bell is clanging.

"That means we had better come ... right now," explains Bill, who doesn't usually obey the rules. We ease back through the bramble path and then run around the vegetable garden and the flower garden and run across the green lawn. "This is where we set up the croquet set. I challenge you," Bill pants.

"O.K. If you don't change the rules in the middle."

"Well, Bill, I'm glad to see you remembered what the bell is for." A smiling face with red cheeks greets us. "And I made your favorite yellow cake to say I'm glad to have you back," Carleen chuckles and wipes her big, red hands on the dish towel. "So this is Eliza. I hope you'll like cats."

"I do like cats, especially kittens. Do you have any kittens?"

"Sure do. Down in the storm cellar. Explore some after lunch."

"Carleen, did you get rid of the snakes that live in the cellar?" Bill questions.

I ignore him. "I like your rock fences, Uncle Henry," I say, "in fact, I like everything." He nods and smiles and taps his pipe.

"Stone walls, not rock fences," chimes in Bill.

"And I like the blueberries, too," I continue.

"Not bloo-ber-ries, it's blue-burees," chimes in Bill again.

"Oh hush, whatever it is, I like it."

"Let me show you your room," intervenes Gamma.

The farm house has three floors. Stairs go straight up from the front door to the second floor. There is Uncle Henry's room, a room for Gamma, a smaller catch-all room, and then mine is the blue room. It is painted light blue and the woodwork is white, and there are white iron twin beds with light blue seersucker bedspreads on them; a flowered curtain hangs for a closet door, and white ruffled curtains are at the two windows that look out front onto the road. A white painted dresser with a mirror made to it stands between the windows. The floor is painted shiny light gray and a braided rug is between the beds and so is a little table with a light. The room has a musty, country smell. It is wonderful. "I'm glad you like it. This room was Lucy's. Uncle Henry added a bathroom. It is under the eaves. Duck your head."

We go through the bedroom door to an attic-like storage space and then there is another door and it opens into a nice bathroom with a bathtub on feet and windows that look out back on the croquet lawn. "I like it. There are so many nooks and crannies."

"Plenty of spiders hiding in there," observes Bill looking innocently at the ceiling.

"Oh, Bill, stop that," laughs Gamma.

"I bet there are snakes in your corn crib," I counter. All the same, I think, I will look around carefully. I'm just not crazy about spiders, but I have learned not to scream when I see one. "What's on the third floor?"

"Carleen and Annie stay there when they come down from the city to help us."

The living room is the best of all. It has a red brick fireplace with a plain white mantel, a flowered carpet on the floor, a big table for games or jigsaw puzzles, and at one end windows that look out on the grape arbor. Under the windows is a black horsehair chaise and at the foot of it, a book case with glass doors. A perfect place for reading mysteries!

Chapter III

FIRST DAY AT SUMMER CAMP

I have never been to summer camp, but Sally and Lawrence have. And now, today, I am going. I had really just as soon stay here at the farm and play with the kittens, but Gamma says Uncle Henry has gone to a lot of trouble to plan day camp for me and I would be unappreciative if I didn't act as though it were the best idea in the world. I wear my new white shorts and a red and white checked shirt and red ribbons on my pony tails and my polished white sandals.

A horn honks. My car pool! My stomach feels queasy. The car is full of smiling faces, but they all belong to people I don't know and they all know each other. And no one is wearing a bow ribbon!

"Girls, this is Eliza; she is visiting her Uncle, Mr. Hart, for the summer. She is from Memphis, Tennessee."

"Hi, Eliza."

"Hey," I reply.

"Hay? That's what you feed the horses," laughs one of the faces. "Where is Memphis? It must be in the South. Say something else."

Gosh, I better make this good. "Hey, y'all. I'm sure glad to see y'all." They all laugh. And I meet Frances, Anna, Caroline and Elizabeth.

Several car pools bring groups of girls to the camp and we sit in a big circle on the ground. Thank goodness we each have a name tag.

We talk about the planned activities: swimming and diving, crafts, story-telling. I'm not too good of a swimmer, but I can swim from one side of the pool to the other. Diving, no. I've never even gone off the side of the pool head first. Crafts? I guess I can do a little, but now story-telling ... that I can do! Maybe camp will be okay.

A bus takes us to go swimming. We go to a *BEACH*, not a swimming pool. It is different from the wide, flat beach behind Uncle Henry's farm: huge rocks jut from the water and the waves crash around them at different times making different sounds and giant, leaping white foam and spray. We are going to *swim here*? How can I swim where there is no side to swim to? I begin to feel sick.

Everybody is in the water. I put one toe in. I hear a voice, "Look at that timid little thing."

Frances comes over to me. She looks super in a two-piece flowered suit. "Eliza, just go down all at once."

The water is freezing and it tastes salty on my lips and it burns my eyes and the ocean bottom is lumpy, not smooth like the pool.

"That's the way!" encourages Frances. "And the salt water helps you float. You do know, don't you, that you can't sink in salt water. You just bob like a cork."

"Oh, honest true? I've never been in the ocean before."

"Honest true I believe you!" Frances laughs. "You're going to like it. Just don't step on a man-of-war. I've got to go. My group is practicing diving today."

I look around for the diving board. I can't find it, so I follow Frances with my eyes. She is swimming out to the rocks ... gigantic rocks jutting up out of the foaming sea. What? Some of the girls are climbing up the biggest rock. No, there are little stairs on the side. They are diving off the rock into the white water below? I feel sick at my stomach again. Am I going to have to do that? I'll die. Those girls, those Yankee girls, are brave, very brave indeed. Well, I better at least put my face in and swim, but how can I tell when I've swum far enough? I might just swim too far away from the campers.

"How do you like your first ocean swim?" asks one of my counselors.

"Oh, it's just fine ... but ... but ... I can't tell how far I'm swimming. There's no side to stop me or tell me when I'm in the deep," I blurt out.

"Of course you can't tell. It is different from a pool, isn't it? Do you open your eyes in the pool and when you come up for air?"

I have had trouble doing that, but now I have no choice. "Yes, and what is a man-of-war?" I *simply have* got to touch bottom.

"A man-of-war is like a jelly fish. It won't hurt you unless you step on it."

"Oh." I put my face in and open my eyes. The salt water does sting a little, but probably not as much as stepping on a jelly fish. I come up to breathe and keep my eyes open. I can see where I am! And I sort of bob like a cork. I'm going to like this just fine. I stop swimming, stand up and look for my counselor.

"Watch out!" she yells, and wham, I am knocked flat and scratch my knees on the sand. I come up with seaweed covering my face, matting my hair and my nose and throat burning with salt water and my bathing suit sagging with heavy sand. "You got hit by a wave! Get your breath and I'll show you how to ride them."

"That poor little southern girl is just a baby. She doesn't know how to do anything. No wonder they lost the Civil War."

Who said that? I'm so covered with seaweed I can't see. And my mouth is so full of sand that I can't even give the rebel yell. What a tacky thing to say. I'll show them. They'll all like me before I go home.

Our car pools don't take us home on Fridays. Uncle Henry has hired a chauffeur and a car to take Gamma, Bill or me any where we cannot walk ... like into the Commons for groceries, or to Church, or to bring me back from camp on Fridays. I picture a colored man with a big smile and wearing a dark suit and a chauffeur's black hat and driving a sleek shiny black car and named James, because that's the way it is in the movies. But our chauffeur is Leroy; he wears baggy tan corduroy pants, and drives his own rattly, two-door green Chevrolet. He's not a colored man and doesn't even have a hat. Leroy doesn't smile much and the car looks bent up on the outside and ratty on the inside. Gamma says we're mighty lucky to have rides whenever we need them. But I'm embarrassed for the campers to see him and his car.

Chapter IV

AUNT LUCY

Saturday, I go spend the day with Aunt Lucy. She has short, gray wiry hair that looks as though the hurricane of '38 hit it. Her light blue cardigan matches her eyes, but not her house dress. Gamma says Yankee women don't primp as much as southern ladies do. But she has a deep, hearty laugh that goes with her size, two friendly golden retrievers, Brandy and Cocoa, and is driven everywhere in a big, four door black Buick with a chauffeur named James! She is Aunt Julia's sister, and she has been saddened by her sister's death, but she is a jolly person and she likes to cheer up Uncle Henry. Gamma says Aunt Lucy has always loved Uncle Henry, even when she was a young girl. But Uncle Henry loved her sister, Julia. That's sad. To give your heart to someone and to have him love, not you, but your sister! I wonder if Aunt Lucy still loves Uncle Henry. Do people that old still hold hands and kiss? I doubt it.

We play every kind of double solitaire. My favorite is 'Sympathy.' We always play with cards that have dogs or cats on the backs. Other times we read; sometimes she reads aloud to me.

Aunt Lucy lives a good drive away from Mallow Marvel Farm on her own apple orchard, known for Baldwin and McIntosh apples. She even has a cellar in the ground to store them for they keep a long time. When he has enough, Jake, who manages the orchard, loads his red Chevy truck and takes the boxes to the wholesale Farmers' Market in Providence.

I love her house. There are shelves and shelves of books and the walls are pale yellow wallpaper covered with pictures of babies, dogs and sailing vessels. The babies and children are her niece and nephews, Lucy, Henry, and Richard. The clipper ship belonged to her sea-captain grandfather. The dogs are hers.

"Tell me a story about the clipper ships."

"You sound just like your mother when she was your age. Well, Grandfather was a sea captain, and he had one ship at first. Whenever he had a successful trip and his cargo sold well, he made an investment. Like the house on Lloyd Avenue in Providence, where Henry and Julia lived. He built that house after a very favorable voyage. That time he brought home pirate treasure as well as a bountiful cargo."

"Pirate treasure?" I gasp.

"Yes. Coins. Silver and gold. And some jewelry. See, this ring I wear on my right hand is a piece Grandfather gave me. He gave Julia one just like it. The stone is blue like the sea and it changes in the light, the way the sea does. I call it Mysterious Blue."

"It's beautiful. May I see it?"

"Of course." She tugs the ring over her knuckle. "I really need to get it enlarged. Arthritis, you see. On my already stubby fingers."

"The stone is a mysterious blue. Why does it sit so high up?"

"That's just the way it's made. Julia's doesn't sit quite that high. Probably they were meant to be worn as a pair. They do sort of fit together."

"Did you or Aunt Julia ever wear them as a pair?"

"Well, you know, I believe we did once. Or rather Julia did. It was the first time your Uncle Henry came to call. She said the rings gave them something to talk about. And they were lovely on her long, graceful fingers. I think your Uncle Henry was bewitched by them," Aunt Lucy laughs, "for he was a steady caller after that."

"Where is Aunt Julia's ring now? She wasn't buried with it on, was she?" I whisper.

"Oh, no, of course not. Probably Henry put it in his safe deposit box or maybe he gave it to his daughter Lucy. Named for me," she adds proudly. "She's coming this summer with her fiancé, Lee. Ask her about the ring then."

"Is there something magic about the rings together?" I ponder.

Chapter V

ELIZA'S 10TH BIRTHDAY

Sunday, we go to the Congregational Church at the Commons. It's different from the Episcopal Church I go to in Memphis. Gamma reminds me that people worship in different ways but we pray to the same God, that He hears us whether we are by the blue Atlantic Ocean or the muddy Mississippi.

A cemetery is beside the small white church. "Come see these funny tombstones," calls Bill.

HERE LIES
ABIGAIL LYONS
THE WIFE
OF MATTHEW LYONS

"What's so funny about that?"
"Look at the one next to it."

HERE LIES
SARAH MIDDLETON
WHO SHOULD HAVE BEEN
THE WIFE OF MATTHEW LYONS

"It is funny, but it's sad, too." I can't stop thinking about Aunt Lucy and how she loved Uncle Henry and how he loved her sister instead of her.

But I can't be sad long. Today is my birthday! July 10th and I am 10! And Momma and Poppa have come to visit! Carleen is baking me a cake with sea blue icing; Uncle Henry says that Lucy is coming for a week's stay; Aunt Lucy is bringing Brandy and Cocoa; and, of course, Bill and Gamma.

Gamma is frying the chicken because she says Carleen doesn't know how to fry chicken properly. In fact, Gamma says that nobody in Little Compton even knows what a frying chicken is. The butcher tries to sell her a hen. She has finally learned to ask for a young, tender broiler and then she fries it the southern way and everybody makes over her and eats up all the chicken.

"Look, Eliza, this week's issue of *Life* is dated July 10. You may keep it," offers Poppa.

I like *Life*. I don't read it all, but I like the pictures and the "Movie of the Week." I love to go to the picture show. Little Compton doesn't have one, but that's all right because Little Compton is so wonderful. But I do wish I had a radio here. I miss *Little Orphan Annie* and *Mr. Keen, Tracer of Lost Persons*. They come on right before dinner. I have my Little Orphan Annie radio code ring and I miss getting the secret messages. Best of all I like *Lux Radio Theatre*.[4] I can even listen to that on a school night, if I have finished all my homework. And it's on tonight! The last Monday until September. *Ruggles of Red Gap* with Charles Laughton and Zazu Pitts. I love the

---

[3] *Lux Radio Theatre: weekly one hour play; produced by Cecil B. DeMille; broadcast from Hollywood's Music Box Theatre on Hollywood Blvd. Always new stars. A play with three 15-minute acts, interviewing between the acts, curtain calls, and of course "Lux spots." Ran from June 1, 1936, to January 22, 1945. Even experienced actors got "Mike Fright" as the play was broadcast to 30 million listeners.*

way it opens, all glittery, on opening night with "Curtain going up!"

My birthday is wonderful! I love my presents! Momma and Poppa give me a white radio which I put on the table by my bed. *Lux Radio Theatre* here I come! Gamma and Bill give me a 6-20 Brownie Junior and a roll of film so I can take snapshots of the farm and the rocks at Warren's Point Beach and my friends at camp. Uncle Henry gives me a book, *Lamb's Tales from Shakespeare*, and he writes inside:

To Eliza at ten
From Great Uncle Hen

Aunt Lucy gives me a double deck of cards with a black Scottie dog on one deck and a white Scottie on the other. Her card says "with love and 'Sympathy,' Aunt Lucy." And Cousin Lucy gives me a diary so I can record, as she says, 'profound thoughts of the coming year.' And sweet Carleen gives me one of her kittens, a grey one. Poppa asks me what kind of train ticket I plan to buy for her.

But best of all, Poppa doesn't yell at Bill.

Chapter VI

DINNER AND THE RINGS AND "PIECES OF EIGHT"

"Cousin Lucy, are you wearing the mysterious blue ring that your mother gave you?" I ask.

"Yes, I am," answers smiling Lucy holding out her slender right hand with bright red nail polish, "but I'm surprised you aren't more interested in the ring on my left hand. I thought girls ten years old liked romance and weddings and things like that."

"Uh, huh," I nod, "but it is mysterious blue and looks even bluer with your blue angora sweater and maybe there is a mystery with yours and Aunt Lucy's rings. Could you each try them on together and see what happens?"

It is so cool tonight that there is a fire in the fireplace in the parlor and in the little grate in the dining room. Sally and Lawrence will never believe me: a fire in July! This is a company dinner so Leroy's son, Gus, is helping Carleen serve. He's not as cheery as she is, I guess more like his father, serious. At least he wears dark trousers that fit.

In addition to Gamma's southern fried chicken, we're having a New England dinner: codfish cakes. They're not sweet cakes, but fried, like salmon croquettes at home, and made with potatoes and cod. Cod is such an important fish here in New England that they named Cape Cod for it. We have Cotton Row in Memphis; it's a street near the Mississippi River where all the cotton businesses are. Also, we're having summer squash casserole; that's what we call yellow squash at home; and fresh asparagus from the vegetable garden. I picked them myself! I forgot, corn oyster stew first. So good! I'm learning to like new things.

While we are seated around the oval dining room table waiting for dessert, Lucy and Aunt Lucy finally get to the matter of the rings. I'm on pins and needles. First, Aunt Lucy puts the two mysterious blue rings on her finger. They look lovely as a pair and they do fit together as if they were meant to be that way. "But I don't see anything strange or unusual; they are just beautiful," says cousin Lucy.

"Eliza, go ask Carleen for a magnifying glass. Maybe there is something we don't see." I dash to the kitchen and Carleen finds the magnifying glass in a jiffy.

"And what'll that be for?" asks Gus, his green eyes almost looking under his eyelids.

"We think the mysterious blue rings hold a secret," I answer quickly, but I feel funny.

"And what kind of secret will that be?" Gus opens his eyes wide.

"We're just playing a game," I reply curtly and hurry back to the dining room. Aunt Lucy pulls the candles closer and examines the rings carefully under the magnifying glass. "Well, look, there is something a little irregular here. There is one extra of these gold perpendiculars on the taller ring. I wonder why that is because everything else about the ring is so symmetrical. Funny I had not noticed that before. What does it do, I wonder."

"A release mechanism," observes Uncle Henry.

Gus is passing the blackberry pie. "What'll that be, Mr. Hart? I'm good at mechanical things. Lemme see the rings." He puts down the pie and rubs his thumb and first finger together.

We all look at Gus and at each other. Suddenly our game is not so much fun. I don't want Gus to take the rings. Uncle Henry taps his pipe slowly and looks Gus straight in the eye. Everything is very quiet. Then Uncle Henry, still looking at Gus straight in the eye says, "Let a good man try."

We all let go our breaths and Gus takes the two rings and the magnifying glass in his restless fingers. "It is a release, Mr. Hart. Look, the top of the taller ring opens!"

Gus' hands are shaking as he gives the rings to Uncle Henry who nods at Gus and passes them to Aunt Lucy. "Lucy, inspect your grandfather's rings."

Aunt Lucy peers inside using the magnifying glass. "There is something in here. I need some tweezers or a straight pin." By now Carleen is at the table with her basket of small household tools.

"Here you are, Miss Lucy. Whatever do you think it'll be?"

We've forgotten the blackberry pie; we are all leaning toward Aunt Lucy, breathless, waiting. She probes first with the tweezers; they are too big. Then the straight pin stabs something and brings it out. A teeny-tiny piece of rolled paper ... tee-nyn-see! Aunt Lucy smoothes it out. Now her hands are shaking. "Does it say something?" we all ask. Aunt Lucy looks up and then she looks at me and smiles, "Eliza, the mysterious blue ring says '8'!"

"Eight? like eight o'clock?" I stammer.

"Or the figure 8, like in ice-skating?" asks Poppa who likes Sonja Henie.

"Or 4x2 or 2+2+2+2 or 2 cubed?" suggests Momma who used to be a math teacher.

"Or pieces of eight? Didn't you say Grandfather got this from a pirate ship?" cousin Lucy's blue eyes are dancing.

"Or playing cards with an 8. There are the four suits with 8's," Aunt Lucy winks at me.

"Or eight something's, like eight clams, or cod or is it cods? Or the wind at 8 knots?" Bill and his sea thoughts.

"I think," says Uncle Henry tapping his pipe, "we are behind the eight ball!"

—⁓—

Next morning, I can hardly wait for my car pool; there is so much to tell. "You'll never guess," I am breathless as I relate the evening before.

Frances says, "I bet your Aunt Lucy planted that little paper in there. I bet she used what my mother calls, 'Miss Conway's lively imagination.'"

"Oh, Franny, would she tease that much? Anna, do you think so? You don't think there was a pirate treasure found by her grandfather Conway?"

"Well, Eliza, you said that Gus was mighty curious. He must have believed the story," Anna observes thoughtfully.

"Miss Conway does read a lot; I think she writes books, too; and she does live alone," whispers Caroline.

"She does not live alone," I retort hotly. "She has Brandy and Cocoa and Rose who lives with her and keeps house and James who is there to drive her. And Jake who runs the apple orchard. Not that it makes any difference if she does live alone ... she is the sweetest, dearest Aunt. She plays 'Sympathy' anytime and she likes to play with me, too." I hold back the tears.

I can't think about the mysterious blue rings because swimming time is so busy. I concentrate on my strokes and breathing and keeping my eyes open and not stepping on a man-of-war. I am getting better and I'll show that person that southern girls can swim in Yankee waters.

At story time, Elizabeth says, "Eliza, tell us more about the mysterious blue rings."

"Do you believe me? Do you really want to know?" Lots of heads nod in agreement, except Jeannine who says under her breath, "Oh boring baby stuff."

"Well, we could do a scavenger hunt looking for things that are '8' and maybe get some more clues." That is agreed upon for the next day, but in the meantime I must tell some more southern stories. "Well, ever-day I goes down to the rivah and sits on a cotton bale and splashes my toes in the mighty Mississippi and sings 'Ol' Man Rivah.'" Frances, Anna, Caroline and Elizabeth believe me.

Am I learning to tease like Bill?

Chapter VII

SOME SCARY THINGS

"Bill, I heard noises like thunder last night and today, off and on, only not thunder. Did you hear them?"

"Yup, it's the coastal defense batteries going off. They're sort of hidden, but I've seen some of them."

"Is that true? What are coastal defense batteries? Are you teasing me?" I almost want to cry. Does that mean a war? I read in the *Life* Poppa left me that there are two million Japanese soldiers in China and the Japanese are training more. Japan has conquered most of China's big cities and the war is not over. China is a long way away though. Like in the war in Spain that ended in April. We have the Atlantic Ocean on one side of us and the Pacific on the other, so I can feel safe. On my new radio, I heard Adolph Hitler making a speech from Germany, but the speech was mostly ranting and screaming. Cousin Lucy has been to school in Germany; in fact, she speaks German and she has actually seen Hitler and heard him speak to a large group. She says he has a kind of power over people and he really is sort of attractive. If Cousin Lucy thinks that, then maybe he's not all bad.

"Tease? Would I tease you?"

"You tease me all the time. You know it!"

"Well, all I know now is I need to get on over to my sailing lesson. Near noontime the prevailing southwesterly winds begin. The people around here call it 'the main event of the coastal day.' There'll be white caps and a haze in the air. But by six o'clock the wind will subside and it'll go to bed with the sun."

But tonight is different; the wind does not subside. It gets louder and the rain is heavy and is slung about and it is downright cold. We have fires in the grates again and then the lights go out. It's a storm! "Is it a hurricane?" I whisper.

"Might very well be," muses Bill. "The hurricane of '38 had a tidal wave that made the water flow to eight feet deep on the streets of Providence. More than 300 people were killed."

"Where'll we go to be safe?" I shiver.

"Really, Eliza, *this* is only a little blow. Nothing to worry about. Why don't you turn on your radio?"

"I can't. There's no power, silly."

"Well, then, we can always take our candles and go to the storm cellar where the snakes and spiders are and tell ghost stories," Bill chuckles.

"Why does nobody believe me? Nobody believes me that there is a mystery about the rings and you don't believe this is a storm? I wish the rings would reveal a secret treasure and you wouldn't get any," I cry in half anger and half frustration. I don't like storms and I don't like spiders and I don't like for people not to believe me or not to tell me what is going on.

I try to call Aunt Lucy on the phone, but the lines are down. I've got to find out if she made up the story of the rings. I finally doze off to sleep on the horsehair sofa, looking out the windows at the storm and with a candle burning on the table at my feet.

Chapter VIII

THE SUMMER IS OVER

The scavenger hunt at camp produces lots of 'eights' that we had not thought of. A calendar page of the month of August, the eighth month, where we are right now; a cup that has eight ounces written on the side; eight clam shells. One lady gives us a picture of her eight children: Momma would say "That's a good catholic family." There are eight cups in half a gallon.

Uncle Henry says his golf handicap is eight. Carleen says she wishes she worked only eight hours a day. There's the chant, "Two, four, six, eight, Who do we appreciate?" There can be 8+8+8+8 and so on or 88 or 888 or 8,888. Or an octave, eight keys on the piano.

We begin to giggle. "I ate all my yams," laughs Franny.

"Hun-nee, it's not yams, it's sweet po-ta-ters," and we laugh till we cry.

It's the last day of camp and I win the award for the most improved at swimming. I know that's right. We hug each other. Except Jeannine who was busy with the paints. I've learned about Yankee girls and they've learned about a southern girl.

—∿∿—

I'm in my pretty blue room, packing and waiting for *Little Orphan Annie* to begin and a news broadcast comes on instead. Nazi Germany and the Communist Soviet Union have signed non-aggression pacts.

That sounds good to me if countries have agreed not to fight, but the announcer's voice doesn't sound glad.

I tell Uncle Henry about the news broadcast. He taps his pipe, looks his same calm look and says, "The political balance of the world has changed."

"Does that mean a war?" I ask, afraid of what he will say but knowing he will tell me the truth.

"Today is August 29th. In another week, we will know."

"In another week? In another week, I'll be home."

It's goodbye to Mallow Marvel Farm and the apple orchard and the stone walls and my kitten, Octavia, and Aunt Lucy and Carleen and the smell of the sea. The candle stick I put on the table at the foot of the horsehair chaise the night of the almost-hurricane is still there. Part of me is still there.

———

We will sail on a boat, a packet, from Providence to New York City! "This is the way we used to travel, by steamer," explains Gamma. "It is not a ship like an ocean liner, but it is big like a house and has a handsome staircase."

"We will be sailing in the dark?" I question.

"Yes, and I know how to rock the boat," chimes in Bill as he leans back and forth holding the railing.

The boat does go up and down! "Stop it, Bill!" I plead.

Gamma continues, "Remember the boat has lights and horns and a skilled captain. And there are lifeboats and a lifeboat drill. And this is a regular run that carries mail and passengers twice a week. And besides, you know how to swim! And surely you know by now your brother is a tease?"

Pulling from the dock and waving at people on the shore is thrilling and the packet steamer is exciting. There is a wide stately staircase with a chandelier and we have dinner and then explore the boat and look at the dark sea from over the rail and see the moon shining on the dark sea. What the sea has come to mean to me this summer! I never thought about it before, when I lived just in Memphis. I love the big muddy Mississippi River, but the sea is different. I think my world has grown. I think that is a profound thought and I shall write about it in my diary.

Chapter X

BACK HOME

Momma and Poppa are at the train station and hug and kiss us like crazy, except Poppa shakes hands with Bill. "Coming home is the best part of any trip," says Gamma, "that's what my mother always said to me and I believe it is true."

The red roses are still blooming on the wallpaper in my bedroom and my spool bed is still covered with the bedspread Gamma crocheted for me. "Every stitch full of love for you," she had said. But somehow my room feels different. I phone Sally and Lawrence. They are coming over. I unpack and plug in my birthday radio and put my Most Improved Swimming Award on my dresser and a picture of Octavia-cat on my mirror. Then, I look for the Sunday funnies. Momma and Poppa are reading the paper downstairs in the sitting room.

"Are we at war?" I ask.

"No, the United States is not," answers Poppa, "but the world situation is grave."

"Adolph Hitler spoke to the Reichstag. That's like our Congress, Eliza. He claimed he would not wage a war against women and children. But as he was speaking, German planes were dropping bombs on women and children in Polish cities," Momma says, her brown eyes filling with tears. "Six hundred fifty thousand children are being evacuated from London. Here's a picture of the mothers weeping at the gates at the train station. The break-up of homes is heart-breaking."

"Breaking-up homes is a tragedy," agrees Poppa, "it would also be one if the children suffered or died in the war; but the greatest tragedy to me is the cycle of war. We thought the 1914-1918 war would end the insanity of killing. Now here we go again. And these children may live through still another cycle."

"Poppa, Hitler says he won't bomb cities."

Poppa folds his paper. "Actually, Eliza, the bombing of cities is inevitable. It is just a fact of war that industrial cities are prime targets to be destroyed."

I feel sick at my stomach.

"Let's turn on the radio and get some news," says Bill.

"It is about time for the news round-up with Ed Murrow," agrees Poppa. "I like hearing the news live, although I still prefer to read the morning and evening papers at my leisure."

For the first time in over a hundred years, the House of Commons is meeting on a Sunday.

Great Britain and France have declared war on Nazi Germany!

The words from the radio settle on the white summer slip covers.

In a moment, President Roosevelt is speaking:

This nation will remain a neutral nation, but I cannot ask that every American remain neutral in thought as well. Even a neutral has a right to take account of facts. Even a neutral cannot be asked to close his mind or his conscience.

"Momma, I know what neutral means, but tell me again."

"It means not taking sides; it also means not assisting any side."

"But isn't it right to side with the good and against the bad? Isn't England good and Nazi Germany bad? Didn't the King and Queen of England visit the United States this June while I was in Rhode Island?"

"Yes, King George VI and Queen Mary did come to visit and I imagine that invitation was to stimulate mutual friendship."

"Well, it did, didn't it? I mean, aren't we friendly? I do think about Princess Elizabeth and Margaret Rose."

"Say, do you know that today all rides at the Fairgrounds are a nickel?" interrupts Bill, looking at the paper. "The gates open at two o'clock."

"You're not really interested in world affairs, Bill?" Poppa has a sour look. He heaves a sigh and turns down the radio and says flatly, "Before you go dashing off someplace, I suggest you both write your thank you notes to Uncle Henry and Aunt Lucy."

"Come on, Eliza, let's get this done." I follow Bill into the sunny breakfast room. "What we can do for Gamma for taking us this summer?"

"Let's see, what does she like? She likes her morning tea. She says it tastes like velvet."

"She likes toast with her morning tea and our toaster is shot. Let's get her a new toaster. I saw an ad that you can trade in an old Toastmaster and get a new one for $2.00."

"That's a super idea."

"Do you have a dollar? I do."

I get fifty cents a week allowance. I have to pay church and movies out of that. We went to church in Little Compton, but there wasn't a picture show "I have a dollar, easy. Of course, I am saving for Christmas, but it is a long way off."

"I'll ride my bike over to the hardware store tomorrow and get it."

I nod and sit down to write Uncle Henry. I try to be as economical as he is with his words.

Chapter X

SALLY AND LAWRENCE AND A LETTER FROM UNCLE HENRY

Monday, Sally and Lawrence and I walk to the Five and Ten Cent Store to buy our school supplies. I love to get a new blue notebook and paper and dividers and composition books and crayons and a bottle of ink. Everything smells like school. I can't wait for the first night there is a cool breeze through my bedroom windows and Momma opens the cedar chest and gets out a blanket that smells like moth balls. Then I can snooky down in my snooky bed and it is wonderful. Sally and Lawrence cannot believe that we had fires in the grates several nights in Little Compton. They believe the ring story though. They think there is a treasure somewhere and that Aunt Lucy would not have pulled that kind of joke on me. They aren't too much worried about the war. I think maybe living close to the ocean makes people more worried.

"We have all that ocean between us and the bad Nazi's. We don't need to think about it. Besides that is England and France's business, not ours," says Sally positively, her brown eyes serious and with a shake of her brown bob.

"You are so tan," I admire. "I just get red and turn back white."

"Well, you are browner than usual," Sally observes. I am so glad to see Sally and Lawrence.

Sally says that her Daddy said that British bombers flew over

Germany last night and instead of dropping bombs, they dropped six million leaflets!

"Were the leaflets in German? What did they say?" I ask.

"Yes, Daddy said they were in German and told the German people that the British people wanted to live in peace with them and that the Nazi government was not telling the German people the truth."

"That sounds like a good idea to me if it would stop a war," observes Lawrence, looking serious even though it's hard to do with one eye green and one eye blue. "I don't have any brothers and my daddy is too old to fight," she adds.

"Same here," nods Sally.

"My poppa is too old and Bill is too young, now, that is. He'll be 14 this week. Surely this won't be going on four years from now."

"Surely not," agree the girls.

"Four years from now, we'll be fourteen!" I say to Sally.

"I know, and I'll be thirteen," smiles Lawrence. "And, I am taller than either one of you."

"Well, let me tell you about the Yankee girls I met. They were all nice except Jeannine and can they swim! But they thought I talked funny!" We all laugh.

"Well, you talk funny now yourself," observes Sally.

That afternoon the evening paper has terrible news: The British ocean liner "Athenia" is sunk, on the first day of the war. There are 1,418 passengers, three-fourths of them are women and children. And some are Americans! The sinking happened at night, at a quarter to eight; I know what the sea looks like at night. They were sailing in uneasy waters off the rocky coast of Ireland; I know what uneasy waters are. The paper says:

A shattering explosion rent 'Athenia's' steel hull. A water spout leapt 70 feet in the air. Promenading passengers were hurled over rails into the sea.

I remember our night on the packet from Providence to New York when we leaned over the rails and looked at the moon on the sea. Oh terror! To be hurled over the rails into the darkest deep! There is more to the newspaper story:

Lifeboats were overloaded, listing, capsizing. There were swimmers, bits of wreckage. Near midnight a Norwegian freighter arrived and took 450 survivors. Other vessels took 376 more survivors. Missing: 126. It is not known how many are Americans.

I shiver with fear and comprehension. What would I have done if that had happened to me? Would I have been brave? At least I can swim now. I can almost taste the salt water in my mouth.

"Eliza, you have a letter!"

From Uncle Henry. He couldn't be answering mine. It hasn't had time to get there.

> Dear Eliza,
>   Octavia is fine, but she misses you. Rose misses you and Bill.
>   An odd thing: we returned to the Providence house for the autumn and found that one of the steps up to the front porch had been tampered with. It was the eighth step! Further investigation is needed.

43

Europe is in blackout for the war and the English are being conscripted: men, ages 18-41. Ten thousand Americans who believed there would be no war have fled Europe on any available space on an ocean liner. Ships are steering a zig-zag course and answering no radio or telegraph messages.

But, to anticipate your question, no, I don't think we will be at war by Christmas.

Come back to see me, you and Bill and Sister.

Love from Uncle Hen.

I feel better. Christmas is a long way away. But why was the eighth step to the front porch of the house on Lloyd Avenue tampered with? Was it just rotten or had somebody pried it loose? Had there been something hidden inside?

Chapter XI

SEPTEMBER AND A NEW SCHOOL

I open my eyes and try to remember what is so special about today. Oh, yes, school starts tomorrow. I jump from my spool bed and hurry down to the stair landing to the phone. "Sally, what can we do today? It's our last day of freedom."

"Eliza, guess what?"

"What?" I ask. Sally sounds excited.

"Mother just told me. I'm going to Miss Meriwether's School! It doesn't start for another week. We can still do something today."

"Gee, Sally, that's super." We've talked about Miss Meriwether's School. About how it is for girls only, and how hard it is, and how you begin Latin in the eighth grade instead of the ninth, and how you take French from kindergarten through the twelfth grade. I'm glad for her but at the same time, I feel left out and sad and jealous. I wish I could go too.

"Sally, that really is neat, but who am I going to walk to school with?" I try to keep the whine that I feel out of my voice.

"Gosh, I don't know. Why don't you ask your mother? I heard my mother talking to her last night on the phone."

"O.K., I'll call you in a little while about today." I put the heavy black receiver back in its cradle. What's so special about today? Yuk! Sally and I won't be walking together anymore. Davis School and

Miss Meriwether's aren't even in the same direction. Sally will make new friends at that school and'll be walking with somebody else and after a while, we won't be best friends anymore. Yuk!

"Eliza? Is that you? I was letting you sleep this morning." Momma's voice comes from downstairs.

"Yes, Momma." I run downstairs. "Momma, Sally's going to Miss Meriwether's School. We won't be walking to school together anymore." I'm holding back the tears. "Sally said to ask you who I would be walking with. That you and her mother were talking last night."

Mother is smiling. Why is she smiling at this news? She has that I've-got-a-secret-look.

"Yes, I was talking to Mrs. Long last night and practically every other day the last few weeks.

Momma's eyes are dancing now. "What about, Momma?"

Momma takes me by the hands. "How would you like to go to Miss Meriwether's School this year?"

"Oh, Momma! Can I? I know it costs a lot."

"Yes, Eliza, Poppa and I think we can manage it, but you must keep your grades up because it is a privilege to go there."

I can't take it all in. I have wanted to go there so badly and then my best friend was going and I wasn't, and now I am going and we can still walk together every day. "Oh, Momma, thank you!" I give her a big hug. "I will keep up my grades. You'll see. I better go call Sally and tell her."

I race back to the stair landing and dial Sally's number as fast as I can. Sally answers on the first ring. "Sally, I'm going too! Momma says that I can go to Miss Meriwether's. That she and your mother have been talking almost every day."

"I know. After Mother told me that I was going and I was glad but not glad, because we wouldn't be walking together, then she had to tell me about you. But she made me promise not to tell you, because she knew your momma wanted the fun of telling you. Isn't it wonderful?"

"We can walk, can't we? It's not too far, is it?" We have so many things to talk about when we walk. It's just not the same in a carpool.

"Yes, we can. But let's not walk the first day."

"No, not the first day. When is the first day?"

"Wednesday the 13th. A week from today."

"I'm glad it's not Friday the 13th." We both laugh at nothing.

Chapter XII

FIRST DAY AT MISS MERIWETHER'S

Wednesday morning, Momma drives me to school in the new robin's egg blue Studebaker. She pulls into the bright blue and white Pure Oil Station on the corner, three doors from Miss Meriwether's School.

"A dollar's worth, please," she says to one uniformed attendant while another one cleans the windshield of our beautiful new car. I'm proud Momma is driving me in the new car. I am so excited that my stomach is turning.

"Five gallons lasts me a week," Momma notes in her car memo book. "Well, goodbye, Eliza. Have a happy first day!"

"Goodbye? Aren't you going to take me to school on my first day?" My mouth is dry; there is nothing to swallow.

"Oh, the school is just three doors up and there are no streets to cross. You'll do fine. Besides, there are some things I must do." Momma starts rummaging in her handbag.

I can hardly breathe. I keep hearing Momma say "Goodbye, Eliza."

The car door is heavy. "Momma, are you sure?" She nods and gives me a "little-engine-that-could smile."

"Yes, you'll do fine. Bye." She waves and drives off.

I walk up the sidewalk. "You'll do fine ... you'll do fine ... you'll do fine." repeats itself in my head. I don't know anybody. I don't know where to go. My heart is thundering. I walk up the steps. Eight? Good gracious! I walk across the grass. This is it. Where do I go?

At the front door there is a green and tan awning held up by poles. A girl is swinging on the poles. I see her, but I don't really look at her.

"Hello. You must be new. My name is Catherine Hunt. I'll show you where to go."

Oh joy! Oh, thank you, God. "My name is Eliza Horton. I'm in the fifth grade." I almost sing it.

"I'm in the fifth grade too," says Catherine. "I'll show you the way. Miss Hughes is our homeroom teacher."

The hall is dark after the bright sun, but I am so happy. I follow her with my heart rejoicing. Catherine has a short haircut and she wears cute sandals. I meet the other girls, but I don't get all the names straight. Sally and I are the only new girls. Sally isn't here yet. We make number 12 and 13.

Oh, here comes Sally! And Mrs. Long. I race up to them. "Hey, Sally."

"Hey," she smiles.

"Hello, Eliza," says Mrs. Long.

"My mother didn't bring me," I blurt out.

Chapter XIII

DEALING WITH THOUGHTLESS WORDS

"Poppa, we have homework the first day!" I hold up a stack of books. "And we buy our own. It's not like at Davis where the books are already in the room. I did get mine second hand though."

"Is that because they have all the answers written in?" cracks Bill.

I give Bill what I hope is a withering look. "Of course not."

Poppa, peers over his glasses and his newspaper, "There's nothing wrong with second hand books if they are in usable condition. I'm glad to hear you are started out with homework. The teachers mean business and I don't mean, monkey-business." He laughs at his own joke. "And I hear you took yourself to a brand new school! That takes courage."

I notice Bill looks impressed. "Yes, Poppa. I did. There was the nicest girl who showed me where to go."

"So the girls weren't as snooty as you thought, huh?" laughs Bill.

"Did Sally like her first day too? I think it is a happy thing that you two girls are doing this together," Poppa has a big smile.

"Oh, Poppa, I did a bad thing."

"How's that?" Poppa puts his paper down.

"When Mrs. Long brought Sally into our homeroom, I told her 'My mother didn't bring me.'" I shiver even remembering. Where had those words come from? Had the other girls heard me? Did they think that was mean? Had I gotten started on the wrong foot?

"Well, that's not bad-bad," says Poppa taking my chin in his hand and making me look at him in the eye. "You spoke without thinking and that nearly always gets us into trouble."

I can't speak without crying, so I just nod.

"I bet you were excited over having entered a new school by yourself and you wanted to tell someone and whom would you rather tell than Sally?"

I nod again. "But, Poppa, it came out mean and braggy."

"I know. Once again that's what happens when we don't think before we speak." He shoots a look at Bill.

"I bet Sally is mad at me."

"Do you really think so? Or are you just cross with yourself? Didn't you all see each other all day at school?"

"Yes, Poppa."

"How many times have you talked on the phone since school?"

"We haven't."

"You haven't? Well, my suggestion is you call her right now."

"What'll I say?"

"I can't tell you exactly what to say, but let her know that you regret those thoughtless words."

"I'll call her after dinner."

"No, call her now."

I'm glad the phone is on the stair landing so that neither Bill nor Poppa can hear me. Sally's line is ringing.

"Hello."

"Hey, Sally,"

"Hey."

"Well, how did you like it?"

"Oh, I liked it, didn't you?"

"Yes. I couldn't get over what the geography teacher, Mrs. Freeland, said."

"Yeah, I couldn't either. Nobody at Davis ever said that kind of thing to us."

"I 'bout fell over. 'Now, my dears and my darlings, we are going to study Europe this year. We shall have much to discuss.' Sally, I'm so sorry I said what I said." I blurt out this last.

The other end of the phone is quiet.

"You know, when I said, 'My mother didn't bring me.'"

"I know. But that's okay."

"Momma just let me out at the Pure Oil Station and said 'Goodbye.' I was scared. And then, this girl, you know Catherine Hunt?"

"The one with the cute sandals?"

"Yes. Well, she was so nice, not snooty or anything and told me her name and said she would show me where to go. I'll never forget her."

"That was definitely not snooty," agrees Sally.

"Poppa said I was so relieved and that you are the first person I would want to tell. But that I didn't think before I spoke. And that means trouble."

"That's what my daddy says too. I mean, about thinking before I speak."

"Anyway, I'm thinking now. And that was a braggy thing to say. And you are my best friend."

"Well, Eliza, it was a big thing to do, to come by yourself. I don't think I could have done it. I don't think Mother could have let me do it. And you are my best friend."

"Shall we walk tomorrow?"

"Oh, yes, we shall have much to discuss," I mimic Mrs. Freeland and then giggle.

Chapter XIV

A SATURDAY

"Minerva? Is that the market man I hear?"

"Yessum," answers Nursey listening and then looking out the window.

"Straw-ber-rees, bloo-ber-rees, and can-na-looo-pee" comes the sing-song chant.

"Please see what he's got."

Minerva, in her grey uniform with white collar and cuffs and a white bib apron, takes two boiling pots with her and goes out to the street. Other neighbors and their cooks are coming and going to the horse and wagon and the market man. "He's got corn and butter beans and tomatoes, too," calls Minerva.

"Get what looks pretty," answers Momma.

Minerva returns with her treasure. Tomatoes, a penny a pound. Corn on the cob, a penny each. Cantalopes, a nickel apiece. Cucumbers, a penny each And a quart of butter beans. Momma counts out the money. "That's about the same prices as Easy Way. Maybe a little less, but I like to buy from the market man."

"Are we having fried chicken for supper, Nursey?"

Minerva nods "Yes" with a smile that shows her gold tooth, "Ain't it Saturday?" I hug her; she pats me back.

Poppa is home from his law office, listening to the radio and looking at National Geographic maps and making his own charts.

"What's happening in the war, Poppa?"

"Not exactly what I had anticipated," muses Poppa. "Londoners and those who live in other cities in Britain are in momentary danger from an air raid. Many underground shelters are ready and sirens can shriek the moment an enemy plane is sighted. But the swarms of German bombers have not come. Where are they?"

Poppa doesn't expect me to answer, for he continues. "However, the submarines have sunk eight British merchant ships."

I can picture the sea, dark and deep. I remember the story of the Athenia's being sunk. And the fires and the people struggling for lifeboats and the terror.

"The subs came close to winning the last war for the Germans. But now, let's talk about the war in the air. Look at this chart I've made, Eliza. Each sticker stands for 500 airplanes. See France has two stickers; England has six stickers representing 3,000 first line planes; and Germany has 12! Six thousand first line planes. More than France and England combined. And her factories are geared to produce 1,000 a month. And actually Germany could produce two or three times that many at any time," says Poppa with authority.

"Why does France have so few planes?" I ask.

"The French design fine planes and they are able to manufacture them, but they are so slow. It is the incompetence of the Air Ministry. They are only producing about 200 a month. They have ordered some from Holland, England and 700 a month from the United States. But if Congress does not revise the Neutrality Act, we cannot send those planes to France. But even if we could, France cannot catch up with the Germans. With the Germans and their mass production."

"Does that mean England and France will lose the war?"

"It's not that simple, Eliza. There are so many aspects to consider: armies themselves; the generals, that is, the kind of leadership the army has; the navies; the leadership of the country itself and of course, the will and fiber of the people."

"Uncle Henry wrote that the British were conscripting men ages 18 to 41. If our country goes to war, you would be too old and Bill would be too young? Right?"

"Right, Sweetie," Poppa smiles at me, "now, isn't this Saturday? Aren't you and your friends going to the picture show?"

"Yes, Poppa. Sally, Lawrence, and I are going to the Linden Circle to see Peter Lorre and Jean Hersholt in *Mr. Moto in Danger Island* and Charles Starrett in *The Man from Sundown* and Wild Bill Hickok in Overland with Kit Carson ...."

"All that for ten cents?" laughs Poppa. "I couldn't sit that long."

"That's not all. There's a cartoon and a musical! Momma is driving us there and Lawrence's mother is picking us up."

"Do you see Lawrence at your new school? She is a year younger, isn't she?"

"I don't see her, Poppa, because she's in the fourth grade and that's part of the lower school. Fifth, sixth, and seventh are the middle school. I'll see her next year though."

"Is Sally spending the night with you?" asks Bill.

"Why do you want to know? What are you up to?"

"I just might put Herman in your bed!" he quips and makes a quick exit.

"We'll just pull back the covers and look. I'm not afraid of Herman," I shout after him. "And if you do, I'll tell Connie Coleman that you have her name written all over your books."

Chapter XV

SPENDING THE NIGHT WITH SUZANNA

"**M**omma, Suzanna told me at school today that she was going to ask her mother if it was alright for me to spend the night Friday. Can I go if her mother says yes?"

"I don't believe I've met Suzanna, have I?"

"She's in my class. She's the smartest girl in the room. She has dark brown hair, darker than mine, and brown eyes and she has the cutest clothes. She wears a different color sweater every day and she has all kinds of white collars to tuck in each sweater. The chauffeur, Ernest, brings her to school every day. She's been at Miss Meriwether's since kindergarten."

"You have spoken about liking her. Is her name Suzanna Sage?"

"Yes, and she has a younger brother, Stephen. Can I, Momma?"

"May I, Eliza."

"May I? Please."

"I guess that will be all right. I would like to speak to Mrs. Sage though sometime when you are talking to Suzanna."

"Oh, thank you, Momma." I run to call Suzanna. "Suzanna, I can come."

"That's super, because my mother says you can. But my mother wants to talk to your mother on the phone."

"My mother said the same thing." We both laugh and get our

mothers on the phone. It is agreed that I am to come home with Suzanna after school Friday and Momma will pick me up after lunch on Saturday.

"Eliza, perhaps you should let Sally know you are not walking home Friday," suggests Momma.

"Yes, Momma." Oh, I hadn't thought of that. The phone rings. "I'll get it," I call out. "Hello."

"Hey, Eliza,"

"Hey, Sally."

"Eliza, I won't be walking home Friday afternoon because I am going somewhere after school," says Sally.

"Oh. Where are you going?" I ask.

"To Margaret's. She asked me to spend the night and I'll go home with her carpool."

"That's nice. She's nice. I am going home with Suzanna. Ernest, the chauffeur, is her carpool."

"That's nice. She's nice and so smart. How long are you going to stay?"

"Momma is picking me up after lunch. We can still go to the picture show."

"Oh, I'm not coming home from Margaret's until after the picture show."

"Oh."

"But I'll talk to you when I get home."

"Okay. See you in the morning. We'll be loaded down with our books and our overnight bags," I say as I hang up the phone. I hadn't thought about our making different friends.

—◈—

Suzanna's house is beautiful. It's two stories like ours. And Suzanna has her own room, too. But her bedroom doors have mirrors on them and she has built-in drawers and cupboards for her clothes. And her clothes are super. She has two pairs of Sunday shoes: one pair of black patent and the other red. Ernest wears a black cap in the day when he drives and at night he puts on a white coat and serves dinner in the dining room. We eat in the dining room Sunday noon, but we eat in the breakfast room on regular nights. Momma says it is too hard on Minerva to have to serve a meal every night. But at Suzanna's house, there is a cook and Ernest and a laundress.

At dinner, Mr. Sage talks about the war. "FDR asked for a repeal of the Neutrality Act's arms embargo in his opening address to Congress yesterday. The Secretary of State is trying to help him get what he wants. Do you know who our Secretary of State is?" and he looks at me.

"No, sir. I don't."

"Do you, Suzanna?"

"I think so, Father. Is it the man from Tennessee, Mr. Cordell Hull?"

"Right. A fine man. A serious man. He served for 22 years as our representative in Congress, then two years as a Senator, and now six as Secretary of State. A real statesman. Eliza, don't you forget. It is important to know the outstanding men from your state."

"Yessir, I'll remember who Mr. Cordell Hull is," I say.

"I read that congressmen are receiving a half a million letters a day from their constituents, beseeching them to 'Keep America Out of the War,'" observes Mrs. Sage.

"If Congress will allow us to sell arms to Great Britain and France, that will keep us out of the war. Just sitting on the sidelines and claiming to be neutral and allowing Nazi Germany to devour whatever Hitler wants is like being an ostrich," Mr. Sage raises his voice.

Mrs. Sage rings the buzzer with her foot. Ernest appears at the swinging door. "We are ready for dessert, Ernest. Please tell Maude that was delicious."

"Thank you for the good dinner, Mrs. Sage," I say after we scrape the last bit of chocolate cake from our glass plates.

"You're welcome, Eliza. It is our pleasure to have you and please tell your mother that you have lovely table manners. Now, are you girls ready for the movie? Have you decided what you want to see?" asks Mrs. Sage. "Do you want to go, dear?" she asks Mr. Sage.

"What are the choices? I'm not sitting through any double feature."

"At the Malco is Ginger Rogers in *Fifth Avenue Girl*, with the news, of course and at the Warner, *Espionage Agent* with Brenda Marshall and Joel McCrea, and the news. So, one is happy and funny the other one is about the last war, but is timely. Do you want to see either one?"

"I guess *Espionage Agent*. We'll see if our country has learned anything from experience."

"It's a relief Father didn't choose the one at the Malco. *Donald Duck and the Sea Scouts* is the short. Father would die."

Chapter XVI

REPORT CARDS

"This is truly the worst day yet of the war. Look at the headlines:"

U.S. TO DEMAND RETURN OF CAPTURED FREIGHTER
BRITISH LOSE FIVE SHIPS

Poppa's voice is heavy.

"Poppa, don't feel sad. I've got a surprise for you," I give him a big smile and a pat on the arm and sit down on his footstool still in the summer white slip cover.

"Oh, you have, have you?" he brightens, "what has my Tootsie got? What's in the hand behind your back?"

"Something that will make you happy," and I hand him the envelope. "My first six weeks report card."

"It must be fine or you wouldn't be offering it to me," Poppa opens the envelope.

"Well, well, well. That is mighty fine. All A's in your subjects and E's in deportment. That does, indeed, make me happy."

"Poppa, it's the best report card in the class. I beat Suzanna."

"Well, good for you! Are you two in a race?"

"No, Poppa, it just happened. Maybe I won't do as well next time."

"Why not? Are you planning not to pay attention or not to complete your home assignments?"

"Of course not, Poppa. It's just that Suzanna is the smartest one in the class. She really is. And I am new. I don't know. I'm glad but I feel funny all the same."

"Did Suzanna say she was angry?"

"No. But she may not know, because we got our cards after the bell rang and we were told not to open them until we were out of the school. But when Mrs. Freeland gave me mine she said, 'Well done, Eliza. The highest in the class.' I don't know whether anybody heard her or not."

"Well, I'll just sign it with pleasure and tell you myself, 'Well done,' and keep up the good work. It is important always to do your best."

"Yes, Poppa. I'm glad to see you smiling. Mrs. Freeland's class is studying current events this week and we each have to bring clippings from *The Commercial Appeal* or the *Press Scimitar* about something, either at home, in Europe, or in Asia, that's going on now. Are you finished with this week's papers, Poppa?"

"Not tonight's, but the rest I am. Sounds like a good assignment."

"Reading something besides the funnies, eh Eliza?" chimes in Bill. "You should get up at four A.M. and fold and toss that morning paper. I bet I know the headlines by heart."

"Having a paper route is a good training ground to learn responsibility, punctuality, and ... " Poppa is interrupted by Bill.

"And the fact that some people don't pay their bills. The Rosses make me come two, three or four times to collect. I know they can afford the paper; they just don't have any change or forget that it's collecting time. I bet I would hear a big howl if I forgot to deliver their paper or if it were late."

"I'm glad the cold weather hasn't started," adds Gamma, "I hate to think of your getting up in the dark and rain and maybe ice. Oh, I almost forgot what I came for: Minerva asked me to tell you that dinner is ready."

Chapter XVII

CURRENT EVENTS AT SCHOOL

"You may go first with your article," and Mrs. Freeland turns to Renee who rises to stand beside her desk.

"Well, everybody knows Mama is French," Renee laughs. We smile with her. Like her Mama, Renee has tight wavy hair and speaks very fast and excitedly. "So, my news is about France."

Renee pronounces it 'Frawnce.' I wonder if she's going to talk about the shortage of French planes. That's about all I know except that our French teacher, Mademoiselle Augustin, says that the French language is the language of culture and of diplomacy and that is why the students at Miss Meriwether's start to learn it in kindergarten.

Renee continues, "And everybody knows the famous French actor, Charles Boyer?"

Sighs and muffled "Oui, oui" emerge from the class.

"Well, the paper said that he's being pulled out of the trenches on the Western Front and will fulfill a propaganda mission in the United States."

"I know we are delighted over Mr. Boyer's safety," agrees Mrs. Freeland, "But Renee's clipping has several significant aspects. First, where is the Western Front? Renee, please pull down the map of Europe."

Mrs. Freeland takes her pointer and shows us the Western Front where the French Maginot Line and the German West Wall run close to each other. "Renee, do you know what 'propaganda' means?"

"Yes, Mrs. Freeland. Charles Boyer's very popular in this country. He will make appearances and speeches and do propaganda on behalf of France. And people will pay more attention to her plight."

"Yes, Renee. Do you know if there is any difference between propaganda and publicity?"

"One is good and the other bad?" asks Renee.

"Well, it is odd, class. If we tell something that will benefit our side, we call it 'good' and if our enemies say something to help themselves, we call it 'bad.' Can you think of any examples recently? Yes, Suzanna?"

"The British dropped propaganda leaflets, instead of bombs, on the German cities saying to the German people that Nazi censorship had withheld the truth from the German people and that they are almost bankrupt and that Britain and her allies were invincible." Suzanna stands at the side of the desk speaking easily. "The British thought that was a smart idea and the Germans didn't like it."

"Right," comments Mrs. Freeland. "Yes, Beverly, you have your hand up?"

Beverly rises to ask, "Why didn't the British drop bombs? Why aren't the Germans bombing England? My daddy says it is a phony war."

"My daddy says ... "

"Wait to be recognized, please, my dears and my darlings. Is that all you want to say, Beverly?"

"Yes, Mrs. Freeland, except I want to know why nothing is going on."

"Yes, Margaret?"

"My daddy says nothing is going on because the leaders don't want to bomb private property of another country. Of course, Hitler bombed Poland, but Poland wasn't strong enough to bomb back." Margaret's long straight black hair is plaited in braids today and they are tied with mousey color ribbons to match her mousey sweater.

"Thank you, Margaret. Yes, Eliza?"

"There is a lot going on at sea. The British battleship "Royal Oak" was sunk by a German U-boat and 800 people were lost. And one of our ships, "City of Flint" was taken to a Russian port by a German raider, and that same day the British lost five ships. It must be terrible to go down at sea."

"Thank you, Eliza. We have only three minutes left, so let us summarize for today and then continue with other reports tomorrow. It seems we are reporting that the war is fierce at sea; there is some fighting on the Western Front; but there is no air war yet. We have not discussed Poland or Russia. And I would like you to look up in your dictionaries and write in your notebooks the definitions of these words: propaganda, publicity, invincible, bankrupt, and Maginot Line. You may work together, if you wish. That is all, my dears, class dismissed."

We stand as Mrs. Freeland leaves the room.

"I wonder if Mrs. Freeland will give me a bad grade if my clipping is about two things in Memphis?" asks Sally.

"She said, 'Either at home or in Europe or Asia.'"

"What are you going to report, Sally? I bet it will be fun," says Margaret. "Of course, yours was a smarty one, Eliza. Do you think you're the only one who has ever seen the sea? And what did you do to get the best report card?"

I can think of nothing to say so I just stare at her fat, freckled face and then at her huge brown oxfords.

Chapter XVIII

MRS. FREELAND'S CLASS TACKLES MORE CURRENT EVENTS

"Good morning, class."

"Good morning, Mrs. Freeland."

"We did not have time for local reports yesterday, so we shall begin with them. Yes, Sally."

"Mr. Crump is running for mayor, but Mr. Chandler will be put in the office."

"Local politics is always a matter for comment. Mr. Crump does run the city and that is not how we learn in our text books that a city should be governed," observes Mrs. Freeland. "What is important is that as you grow up you learn the issues and make intelligent choices at the polls when you vote, and that you serve your city in some way. Anything else, Sally?"

"Yes, Mrs. Freeland. Two things, both about buildings. We have a new apartment building in our neighborhood. It cost a half a million dollars to build and has 96 apartments on eight floors. I think it would be very glamorous to live in an apartment. The other building is a slum clearance project. It's not in my neighborhood; it has 49 apartments. The paper didn't say how much it cost."

"It is good for the economy to have construction going on, because that gives people jobs," observes Mrs. Freeland. "And Sally, your two examples are interesting, because the first one is privately owned and the second is owned by the city. Anyone else with something from our city?"

Marylane rises and walks to the front of the room and holds up her clipping which she has pasted on a piece of cardboard so we can pass it around. "Since there is so much bad in the news right now, I thought this was a happy thing. I will pass around this picture of five children in different public schools and this is what it says:

These children play happily together without a thought of old world hatreds: one has a Greek father, one a father from Switzerland, one, grandparents from Italy, one, grandparents from Germany, one whose father still lives in Poland and one whose father was born in Russia."

"Thank you, Marylane. What questions does this picture raise in your minds, class?"

"Are there any foreign students here, at Miss Meriwether's?" asks Beverly.

"The article does not say that these are foreign students, Beverly, only that their parents or grandparents came from foreign countries."

"And you all know that my mother is French," says Renee quietly.

"These children are from different public schools. How do they know each other? Did this really happen or was it a posed picture?" Suzanna rises to ask.

"Excellent question in view of our vocabulary words for today, Suzanna. Can you give us your judgment of whether this is publicity or propaganda or plain truth?" Mrs. Freeland warms to the day's lesson.

"Well, it could be plain truth. I mean, that these children know each other and play together. But the article doesn't say that they know each other, just that they play happily together. But since they are from different schools, probably it was posed. Did somebody on the newspaper want to speak for peace? If so, I guess it is 'publicity' or 'propaganda.' If you wanted America to get involved with the war, you might say it was 'propaganda.' If you wanted to guide American feelings to concern for all children and their families, then you might call it good 'publicity.' Suzanna sits down.

"Let's make those two words a little clearer: publicity refers to any effort to attract public attention, whether through regular news channels or through paid advertising. Propaganda is a stronger word and suggests the manipulation of public opinion whether through acceptable educational means or through direct or coercive indoctrination," Mrs. Freeland writes these on the black board.

Suzanna raises her hand, "I see the difference. That picture and article would be propaganda because the writer and photographer were trying to manipulate public opinion; however, it was through acceptable means."

"Excellent, Suzanna. The point is, class, to question what you read or see in newspapers, books, or movies, even newsreels."

"Yes, Sally?"

"I saw an ad for a wallpaper sale. Ten cents a roll and 29 cents a roll. There probably weren't many ten cent rolls, right?"

"One way to find out is to go see," quips Catherine.

"Fine class discussion today, my dears. Remember, I told you that it is good to start the habit early of doing some service for your city. Well, this is Community Chest month. We raise money to support agencies in the city that help our poor and needy. All over the city tomorrow people who have given money to the community chest will be wearing a red feather. Shall we take up contributions from our geography class?"

A murmuring of "yes's" and Mrs. Freeland continues, "Do I have two volunteers to be the chairmen?"

Margaret's hand goes up, "Yes. Sally and I will do it. Won't we, Sally?"

Sally looks surprised, but nods "yes."

"Fine. Come to my room first thing tomorrow and I'll give you chairmen your hats to wear and the feathers to distribute. Do you think we can be 100 per cent?" asks Mrs. Freeland as she rises to signal the end of class.

"Sally and I are concerned about our city and about what goes on here. We need to look after our own and not be spending time or money on people and countries across the ocean," Margaret gives me a look as she picks up her books and shoves her way in front of me. "Come on, Sally."

Chapter XIX

RED SHOES

"Gamma will stay with you and Lawrence tonight. Mr. and Mrs. Ross are going with us to the Auditorium to hear Mr. Kaltenborn speak," Momma says as she looks up from her pencil and paper.

"Is Bill going to be here too?" I ask, watching him from the corner of my eye.

"If it bothers you so, I just might stay home," he threatens.

"I don't care if you do; I don't care if you don't. Just leave us alone. Momma, make him leave us alone."

"I think maybe you started this one, Eliza."

"Well, I hope he goes out with his friends."

"You know, someday you'll think his friends are attractive," smiles Mother with her I-know-best look.

Lawrence comes after supper with her suitcase and her new Monopoly game. "Hey, Gamma," she gives Gamma a hug. "Is it too dark to sit on the porch and play? The whole neighborhood missed you this summer."

Gamma looks as happy as when she first tastes her morning tea. "Thank you, Lawrence. What a lovely thing to say."

"If it's too dark to see to play, maybe you can sing 'Froggie.'"

Gamma, smiling, sits on the porch glider and starts humming and then singing 'Froggie went a-courting, he did ride.' We know it by heart, but when she gets to the end, "Now, the bridle and the saddle lie on the shelf, the bridle and the saddle lie on the shelf, if you want anymore, you can sing it yourself. I want some more, but I don't know it. I want some _____, but I ain't got a bit", we supply the blank. Sometimes it's chicken; sometimes it's ice-cream. Tonight we don't seem to know what we want.

"You have to be able to say what you want or you won't get anything," warns Gamma.

"I would say some angel food cake, but that would be cheating because I smelled it when I came in," says Lawrence.

"Well, I would like a pair of red shoes for Sunday," I decide. "Like Suzanna's."

"Oh, yes," agrees Lawrence, "but they wouldn't go with everything."

"I don't care. I just want some red shoes."

We come in from the chilly night air, which Gamma loves, and settle down to Monopoly. Whoever gets Park Place and Boardwalk wins, but we play until bedtime anyway.

I am awakened by Momma's and Poppa's voices in the upstairs hall. "Do you agree with Kaltenborn that the Allies share blame for the war, along with Hitler?" Momma asks Poppa.

"Kaltenborn made his point well, I think, that the policy of appeasement, of giving away someone else's property, was encouraging to Hitler and therefore fatal. Through all the crises, Britain and France failed to act, and Hitler got concessions which Republican Germany had never been able to get. The Saarland, Czechoslovakia,..."

"But that does not mean that we must go to war?" Momma's voice trembles.

"No, I don't think so. Mr. Kalternborn pointed out that while

Germany has had some success, there is nothing to indicate a German victory. There is a stalemate on the Western Front and a blockade at sea. Which side can afford to wait? Why, the Allies, of course," says Poppa, answering his own question. "Germany is facing a shortage of food stuffs, and Russia cannot be of too much help unless she plans to starve herself. But, no matter what, we must not join with Russia. We must not join with the Communists! I agree with Kaltenborn that the greatest danger to the peace of Europe lies in the extension of Russian Communism."

I fall back to sleep and dream I am running, running in my red shoes.

Chapter XX

GAMMA SHOOS POPPA TO THE BIRD FEEDER

"I don't see how the president can just decide when he wants to have Thanksgiving Day and move it," I say.

"That man is crazy, I told you," Poppa looks over his glasses and winks.

"Well, that is not exactly the case. The governor of each state decides for that state. In fact, about half the states will celebrate on November 23 and about half on the 30th. Three states were neutral: Colorado, Mississippi and Texas and they will celebrate twice!" Momma laughs as she crosses her legs. I notice her new high heel black shoes.

"Bet the turkeys don't like that," quips Bill, "but I would."

"I don't imagine Minerva would relish cooking two Thanksgiving dinners," observes Momma. "Anyhow, there's nothing sacred about the date. Many years it has not been on the last Thursday of the month. Actually being on the third Thursday will give me more time to prepare for Christmas."

"That was the idea anyway. According to the Secretary of Commerce, Mr. Hopkins. The new date enables the public to go Christmas shopping more easily and with less frenzy and fuss. And will probably lead to more business," Poppa acknowledges.

"So which one has our governor chosen?"

"The 30th, of course."

"Well, today is only the first of November, so it's still a long way off," I say.

Gamma can no longer keep quiet, "Do you know Mrs. Roosevelt was here yesterday?"

"O my, I think I need to fill the bird feeders," says Poppa leaving the room in a rush.

Gamma watches him leave and smiles. "Eliza, she came on the train and she wore a black crepe frock and a black felt hat and a wine wool coat."

"She knew to wear something dark on the train, didn't she, Gamma? Why was she here in Memphis?"

"Actually she came to visit five farms near Millington. I have the article and picture right here. The photographer wanted her to pose beside some mules and hold the reins. And she refused! Because she said she never does anything make believe."

"That would have been a propaganda pose, wouldn't it? Trying to get people to think she knew about mules," I am pleased with myself.

"She said that she did not come to make a speech, but she actually did. Let me read what she said:

I came to see what you people are doing ... to see a community like this making good financially ....

Since war has come, however, many people are ... wondering whether war will stop our farm programs.

To go on solving our own problems in this country is one of the most important things we can do ....

What's happening in Europe does concern us, of course. But it concerns us more to solve our own problems.

Mrs. Roosevelt personally inspected the farms and homes of five tenants on the project," Gamma continues. "She wanted to know how many in each family; she asked about fuel and livestock, and living conditions. She picked up quilts and climbed ladders to their lofts and said she was much impressed with the type of people and what they were doing. Isn't she a wonderful woman?" Gamma's face is one big smile.

"Sounds so to me, Gamma. Do you suppose she'll write about being here in her "MY DAY" column?"

"I'll see tomorrow," Gamma folds away the clippings. "You can tell your Poppa that he can come back from the bird feeder now," she chuckles as she heads upstairs.

Chapter XXI

MAKING CHRISTMAS LISTS

"Sally, come over after school and let's make our Christmas lists," I say.

"Super idea. Then maybe we could go to town on the bus Saturday and do our shopping."

We spread our money on the living room oriental rug. "I have $8.05 and if I don't go to the movie in December, I could have a $1.00 more."

"Well, you don't have it now," says Sally. "My daddy says you can't spend money if you don't have it in your pocket."

"My daddy says that too," I agree.

"I've got $8.50," counts Sally.

"Who's on your list, Sally?"

"Mamma and Daddy. And Lucille. Do we give presents to last year's friends at Davis? We really haven't seen them but one Saturday."

"Probably not, I guess. But, we could send them each a card. We could both sign it."

"Well," says Sally, thinking all this through, "we could get a cute card with two puppies or two somethings on it and send it early and say that we hope we could go to the movie one day during Christmas vacation. That way we would send a card and maybe get to see some of them and stretch our money."

"And then if I asked Poppa to mail them for us, we wouldn't have to buy the three-cent stamps!"

"My daddy could mail half and your poppa half," Sally suggests.

"That's settled then. We can look for cards tomorrow at Gerber's or Kresses. What about our new classmates? Of course, I want to give a present to Suzanna and Catherine Hunt," I say as I write down our decisions.

"I would get a gift for Margaret. She has had me over several times, and for Renee and for Marylane."

"I like them, too. Although, I don't think Margaret likes me. She's always saying something mean. I don't know that I've done anything to make her mad at me," I wonder out loud. "Has she ever told you that she doesn't like me?" I watch Sally's face.

Sally re-arranges her money. "I don't know," she answers quietly. "But it is hard to choose who to give presents to. Do you think we should get a gift for everyone in the class? There're only eleven, not counting us."

"What could we find that wouldn't cost too much? I've got Momma and Poppa, Bill and Gamma and Minerva and you and Lawrence, of course. One thing I saw in the paper was a box of six pencils with your name stamped in gold for 25¢. For eleven people that would be $2.75 and if I got you one too that would be $3.00."

"We could give them together and say from "the new girls" and then it would only cost us half, which would be $1.38. And the names would show that we thought about them early."

"That's a neat idea, Sally. Would we deliver them at school or ask our mothers to drive us to their houses. I really would like to see where everybody lives."

"Since we are giving a present to everyone, we could take them to school. But then do you think everybody in the class would feel they had to give us presents?"

"I hadn't thought about that. That's not good to think you have to buy someone a present. What else could we do?"

"Oh, listen, listen. I just had a great idea! Sort of like what we are going to say on our cards to our friends at Davis."

"You mean about seeing them at the picture show?"

"Yes, we could have a picture show party together! That's 10¢ admission and we could even let everyone buy one candy bar and one sack of popcorn and that would be 10¢ more. That's 20¢ times 11 ...."

"No, that's 20¢ times 13. We would be going, wouldn't we?" laughs Sally.

"Right, of course, how silly of me. That's 20¢ times 13 which is $2.60, and if we split it, it's just $1.30 apiece. Less than if we split the pencils and then, nobody feels they have to go get us a present."

"And besides that, won't it be fun?"

"Oh, yes! Wait, we've got to get our mothers to drive."

"Well, they don't usually mind if one takes and one picks up."

"But with thirteen of us they would both have to drive both ways."

"Let's go ask them."

"No, I'd rather ask Momma tonight when I am looking at her."

"Good idea. We'll both ask our mothers tonight and then call each other. Oh, what a neat idea!"

"Now for the rest of our lists," I say picking up my pencil. "I think I know what I want to get Momma. A Tic-Tac-Toe three lipstick kit. It has a Robin Hood red, a wine shade and a pink shade and it's at Gerber's and it costs a dollar."

"That's super!" Sally agrees. "Do you mind if I copy you? Mama would like that."

"Of course I don't mind. I don't know what to get Poppa though. He is harder to shop for."

"There is always a tie or some socks or handkerchiefs," suggests Sally. "Or does your Poppa play golf?"

"No, he used to play but he doesn't now. And I don't want to get him socks or handkerchiefs or a tie. Wouldn't you hate to just get that sort of stuff under the tree?"

"Where is your paper? There were lots of gift ideas in the paper yesterday."

"Find Gerber's ad because we're going there anyway to get the lipsticks."

"There are several pages of Gerber's ads ... look a silk muffler for a man, that looks beautiful and it's $1.00. What do you think for our daddys?"

"Super! And look, a double deck of bridge cards for $1.00. That would be perfect for Gamma. And here's a pen and pencil set with your name put on it for $1.00. That's a neat gift!"

"Are you thinking about your brother? Or would he rather have these three Decca records for $1.00. It's a special: one is Bob Crosby singing 'O You Crazy Moon' and 'Melancholy Mood', and one is Jimmy Dorsey, 'A Man and His Dream' and 'Go Hunt A Kite' and the third one is Bing Crosby singing 'Still the Bluebird Sings' and 'An Apple for the Teacher'."

"Oh, Sally, speaking of teacher, do you think we should get Mrs. Freeland a present? I wonder if Meriwether girls give their teachers gifts?"

"I don't know. And of course, we have more teachers than just Mrs. Freeland, but she is different somehow. But I don't think we can give one and not another. And we can't very well take them to the movie!" Sally laughs.

"Now, wait, I'm thinking too many things. The records sound better to me than the pen and pencil set for Bill. I think he would really like that and it might keep him busy listening to records and not bothering us," I observe. "That really is a super idea! And, well, what do you want, Sally?"

"Oh, I don't know. Surprise me!

"O.K., I will. It is always fun to shop for your present."

"It's the first one I open on Christmas."

"If you haven't peeked before!"

"Well, how is your money, Eliza? We've not chosen for Lucille or Minerva."

"I know. And I want to get Nursey something really nice. Momma is getting her sheets and towels because we're supposed to make this a Cotton Christmas to help the farmers. Momma is sending sheets and towels to Uncle Henry and the same to Aunt Lucy. Oh, I've got it! I could get Nursey a really pretty pair of pillow cases, maybe embroidered in blue. She loves blue."

"That's a good idea. I might do the same for Lucille, but she likes pink. Maybe Mama is getting her sheets and towels too."

"I think I'll get Lawrence the pencils with her name. Now, let me see if I have enough money." I write:

```
1/2 of movie for class.............$1.30
3 lipsticks for Momma ............1.00
silk muffler for Poppa .............1.00
3 records for Bill ......................1.00
bridge cards for Gamma .........1.00
pillowcases for Nursey..............???
pencils with name: Lawrence ...25
1/2 of Christmas cards...............50
Sally's surprise ...........................??

Total.................. .................$6.05
```

"I've got it! That leaves me $2.00 for yours and Nursey's presents. But wait, I don't have bus fare to town."

"Eliza, I heard Lucille saying that all bus rides to town are free on Friday. The Christmas parade is that night. Daddy said that was to get everybody to town to shop and then stay to eat and see the parade."

"Well, let's go on Friday after school. Then, maybe you can spend the night and we can write our cards and address them and maybe wrap some presents, if Momma has some wrapping paper. I hope she has some new and not just that saved from last year. I wish she would buy blue tissue paper and get silver ribbon and silver stars with glitter on them. Wouldn't that make a beautiful package. Oh, Sally, don't you just love Christmas?"

Chapter XXII

SPENDING THE NIGHT WITH CATHERINE HUNT

Momma turns in the great iron gate and follows the brick driveway. "Catherine said to drive all the way around. That the front door was in the back," I say as I stare at the wide lawns and oak trees and gardens of yellow flowers. And the tall, mysterious house. "It's a mansion!" I whisper.

"People live in different kinds of houses, Eliza, but people are people and houses don't change that. Have a happy time and watch your table manners," are Mother's parting words as Catherine opens the heavy oak door and comes bounding out, her hair cut bouncing but falling back in the right place.

"I've been watching for you. I'm so glad you could come," Catherine takes my bag. "We'll put this in my room and then I'll show you the house."

My dirty saddle shoes squeak on the marble floor. The entrance hall is huge. The black and white marble squares go on and on. And the staircase! Wide, wide and going up so high. Wouldn't it be super to sweep down, dressed in a trailing red velvet gown and holding a lighted candelabra? The upstairs hall goes on forever too. We go down some little steps and then Catherine opens the door to her room. It has a small fireplace and a window seat and windows with little tiny panes that shine. She has twin beds with squashy, shiny pale peach puffs on them.

"Catherine, is that your guest?"

"Yes, Mrs. Muzzy-dear. This is Eliza Horton. She is in my class at school."

"How do you do, Eliza."

"Just fine, thank you, Mrs. Muzzy-dear," I feel as though I should curtsey, like in the movie, *Catherine and Essex*. "This is certainly a beautiful house."

"Yes, indeed, it is, Eliza. Catherine, your father and mother will be dining in this evening and they have requested that Daphne and Robert and you and your guest join them. Dinner will be served at half after seven. I will tell you when to dress for dinner and then I am given the rest of the evening off." And tiny Mrs. Muzzy-dear, wearing lavender color and lavender scent and with blue lavender hair, leaves the room.

"Catherine, what does she mean 'dress for dinner'?" And I look down at my plaid school skirt and sweater and dirty saddle shoes.

"If we eat in the dining room with Mother and Father, we change from our school clothes. But I didn't know they would be dining-in. I thought we would eat earlier in the breakfast room," Catherine sounds as distressed as I feel.

"Momma could bring me my Sunday clothes. May I use your phone?"

Catherine nods 'yes' and takes me to a phone right outside her room. I dial and the phone rings and rings and then Gamma's voice says, "Hello?"

"Gamma, let me speak to Momma, please,"

"She and your Poppa have gone to play cards at the Saunders'. Is anything the matter?"

"Gamma, Catherine's family wear their Sunday clothes to eat dinner and I came in my school clothes. I was hoping Momma could bring me my Sunday clothes."

"The Saunders live way out, too far for you to ask your Momma to drive in," Gamma sounds concerned. "Wait a minute, I have an idea," and Gamma leaves the phone.

"I'd be glad to lend you something of mine, but I'm so much taller that the skirt would drag the ground. I have such long legs," Catherine adds with a sigh.

"I've always wished mine were long. You win all the races at school," I observe. And, I think to myself, your hair never messes up.

Gamma returns to the phone. "Hello, Eliza. Are you still there? Bill says he'll be glad to ride his bike over and bring you your Sunday dress and shoes."

"Oh, Gamma, what a good idea you had! And Bill said he would do that?" I sigh with relief. "That is super! Tell him to ride around the back to the front door and we'll watch for him."

"It's great to have a big brother who does things for you like that," Catherine observes. "Robert is usually away at school. Come on, there's time to show you the rest of the house before your brother gets here. This is the guest suite," and Catherine points to an alcove from which there are two doors.

"It's beautiful," I exclaim as I look at a bedroom with twin beds and pale blue satin comforters, an adjoining bathroom with a mirrored dressing table with silver comb and brush and then, a sitting room with its own telephone.

"And this is Mother's suite and this is Father's."

"Oh."

"And Robert's room is down that wing. Daphne's room is near mine and Mrs. Muzzy-dear sleeps in there. Let's go downstairs."

The drawing room has a grand piano and a huge fireplace and heavy draperies and matching Chinese vases. The library is large too, but it is cozy with books and a roaring fire and a Victrola that plays a stack of records.

"Let me show you the secret passageway," Catherine motions with her finger.

"Honest true?"

"Yes. Look, see this panel. It looks just like the one on the other side of the front door, near the cloak closet. Well, lean here and push here ...."

"It opens! Oh, I love it! Where does it go?"

"It goes up some tiny winding stairs, but Mother has asked us not to play here because it is so dark and narrow. There's no light in here."

Again I picture myself sweeping down the grand stair case with candlelabra in hand and maybe escaping up these little steps if danger lurked nearby.

"Catherine, where does it go?"

"It doesn't go anywhere now. Father says it has been sealed up. Oh, what was that? Thunder? Are we going to have a storm?"

A storm in this mansion! I shiver with delight and see the lightning through the library windows and the rain slashing down and the fire dancing even brighter.

The door chimes. "Oh, I almost forgot, I am supposed to be watching for Bill."

James is opening the door and I hear him say, "Did you not see the sign, boy? All deliveries to the side door."

"Wait, James, that is Eliza's brother, bringing her clothes for dinner."

"Excuse me, Miss Catherine. Won't you come in, Eliza's brother," he says with a smile.

Bill is dripping from head to foot and my Sunday dress and shoes ... where are they?

Chapter XXIII

DINING-IN AT THE MANSION

"**I**'m too wet to come in," croaks a dripping Bill, "but, Eliza, here are your dress and shoes, and he unzips his jacket and hands me a rolled up package, hardly damp at all.

"And who is this, Catherine?" Mrs. Hunt appears in a long gown, sweeping down the last steps, "Where is James?"

"Mother, this is Bill, Eliza's brother. He was bringing Eliza her dress to wear to dinner."

"Come in, Bill. What a gallant thing to do for your sister! You must be cold. Catherine, you and Eliza take Bill to the fire in the kitchen and get him dry and warm. I'm sure Robert has some clothes that will fit him. You must stay for dinner, Bill. Or is it William? Mr. Hunt will certainly want to meet a young man who is willing to brave a storm on a bicycle to bring his sister her dinner clothes. You will stay, won't you?"

Bill questions me with his eyes.

"Yes, Bill, please stay," I say.

"That's settled then," smiles Mrs. Hunt. "James, please tell the cook to set another place," she sweeps down the three steps to the library.

The kitchen smells wonderful. And it is so big. A fire is roaring and two people are preparing dinner. A bell rings. I look up to see, high on the wall, a glass box with bells and numbers beside them. "That is the library," observes James. "That will be Mr. Hunt wanting his whiskey," and he hastens through the butler's pantry.

Bill gets warm and dry. Mrs. Muzzy-dear and Robert find Bill some clothes and Zora presses my Sunday dress. At the stroke of half after seven we are all combed and ready for dinner.

A heavy brass chandelier gleams over a gigantic table, set with a fine linen cloth and silver and heavy crystal goblets and candles sparkling on either side of the centerpiece of fresh flowers. And candles on the side board and on the wall! It is like in the movies. I watch to see what Catherine does. I hope Bill watches Robert.

Mr. Hunt pulls the chair back for Mrs. Hunt; Robert comes over to pull back a chair and Catherine nods quickly at me. Bill looks around at Catherine and Daphne, still standing. My heart is pounding.

"Daphne, this place is yours?" and Bill gives her a smile and a slight bow. "And, Catherine, am I lucky enough to get to sit by you?"

I can't believe my ears! Is this the same brother who puts Herman in my bath tub?

Mr. Hunt asks the blessing and James brings the soup. "William, I understand you are the hero of the night. Is that so?"

"Well, yessir, no-sir. I mean it was all my grandmother's idea."

"Oh," I interrupt, "Bill, we forgot to call Gamma and tell her what happened to you."

"You may be excused to make the call, William. It is important that parents and grandparents not be anxious when anxiety can be prevented."

"Daphne, tell us your analysis of the Russian attack on Finland."

"Well, Father, Russia had no business attacking Finland. The attack seems to be entirely unprovoked. Red planes are bombing Finland. The Russian army outnumbers the Finnish two to one."

"How are the Finns defending themselves?" continues Mr. Hunt.

"Oh, Father, they are wonderful and so brave and resourceful. Their uniforms are white so they blend in with the snow, and often the troops are on skis and can maneuver quickly over the uneven terrain. They have a new Finnish weapon called 'machine pistols' that can fire 250 rounds a minute."

"What good is a pistol against an entire Russian army?" asks Catherine.

"The paper said that small detachments of 150 men each are divided into mobile units of six men who dart through the forests and mow down the Russians at close range. Can't you just picture it?" Daphne's face is bright with admiration.

"Robert, how serious do you judge the Russian attack on Finland to be?"

Robert clears his throat. Goodness gracious, is Mr. Hunt is going to call on Bill and me? Is this a part of 'dining-in'? However, I am remembering to keep my left hand in my lap and eat my soup without making any noise.

"Well, Father, these successes are, indeed, admirable, but Finland's plight is serious. Her border is 750 miles long and that is a long border to have to defend. And their army is only 200,000 with 100,000 as volunteers. Some foreign observers say that Russia has one million men on Finland's borders."

"Very nice, Daphne and Robert. Don't you agree, my dear?"

"I do indeed. I can also identify with Daphne's admiration for the resourcefulness of the Finns. Like the Dutch who are breaking some dikes and flooding a wide area to halt the Nazis."

"Eliza, do either you or William have anything you would like to add to the discussion? Perhaps about the comparison of Russia and Finland at sea?"

Chapter XXIV

BILL, TWICE AGAIN A HERO

Bill and I look at each other. I don't say anything. Bill puts down his soup spoon, clears his throat, and speaks, "Finland has a tiny navy, but they do have many fishing trawlers and they are superior seamen, as they are marksmen."

I breathe again.

"Do you know anything about the Russian navy?" queries Mr. Hunt, looking at Bill with interest.

"Only their fleet on the Baltic Sea, sir. But, I guess that's the fleet that would concern Finland. The Russians have two battleships, an aircraft cruiser, two modern heavy cruisers, 17 torpedo boats and more than 50 submarines."

Wow! Is that my brother?

"I think God is concerned about Finland, too. A snowstorm has helped stop the invading Soviet troops," adds Mrs. Hunt. "And the Finns have asked for foreign aid, and the League of Nations was summoned in answer to Finland's appeal."

"The League of Nations concept is noble, but I can't see that it can accomplish anything except to issue an ultimatum. And the Russian bear is not going to be impressed with that. What the Finns need is our cold, hard cash. They have paid every installment on their debt from World War I on time. The next payment is due shortly. On

December 15th, to be precise. We should declare a moratorium on that whole debt and extend further credits to her, NOW," Mr. Hunt speaks with command.

"I know we all admire brave Finland, but why the urgency, Father?" asks Daphne.

"Remember your dominoes, Daphne. Just as the fall of Austria made Czechoslovakia indefensible, so the fall of Czechoslovakia made Poland indefensible, so the fall of Finland would make Scandinavia indefensible. And then Stalin would have ports on the Atlantic."

James is passing the roast surrounded by stuffed baked potatoes and Zora comes behind him with a tray of bright vegetables in a design. I'm sure Bill is glad he stayed for dinner even though I'm afraid we'll be called on again. Thank goodness for Mrs. Freeland's geography class.

"There is some news besides the war," Mrs. Hunt smiles approval at James and Zora as they leave the dining room. "The premiere of *Gone With the Wind* is in Atlanta a week from tonight. I have read the book and I am eager to see how the English actress, Vivien Leigh, manages a southern accent."

"Are you and Father going to the premiere?" asks Catherine.

"I think not, Catherine. Your father has business to attend to in New York."

"It would be so exciting to go. Is there any chance you could take Daphne or me?" Catherine gently requests.

"I had not really thought about it. Do you need me to accompany you to New York, Edward?" asks Mrs. Hunt.

"I always like your company, Elise, but this is a very brief trip. I am flying up and I don't believe you would even have time to shop."

"Well, then, Catherine, you have a good idea. But our invitation was only for two. I cannot take both you and Daphne. Daphne, you are the older. Would you like to go next Friday?"

Catherine and I scarcely breathe.

"Mother, dear, I would love to accompany you and be in the glamour of a premiere, but that is the evening of our Junior Cotillion Holiday Ball.

"Of course, and you have the beautiful new white gown to wear. Catherine, do you think you could complete your homework and be able to miss a day of school?" Mrs. Hunt questions.

"Oh, yes, Mother. Yes!" Catherine tries to control her voice.

"I'll help you with the homework," I whisper.

James removes my dinner plate and puts a bowl of clear liquid in front of me. What is it? A dessert soup? It is in a crystal bowl and on a paper doily and that is on a beautiful plate. What do I do with it? I sneak a peep at Bill. He has put his fingers in the bowl! And now he is wiping his hands on his napkin! Oh gracious, I can't look! Maybe nobody else saw him. I pick up my spoon to taste the clear dessert, when Bill says, "Mrs. Hunt, these are the most handsome finger bowls I have ever seen. Did you buy them in New York?"

I quickly put my spoon back on the table. I hope nobody besides Bill saw me. My brother has saved me twice tonight.

A beautiful dessert is passed by James and Zora. The 'dining-in' is over!

Mr. Hunt pulls back Mrs. Hunt's chair; Robert does the same for me; and Bill takes care of Daphne and Catherine, in that order. "Mrs. Hunt, thank you for a delicious dinner. I think it was lucky for me that I got caught in the storm. Mr. Hunt, I profited from your keen knowledge of current events. If it has stopped raining, I should head home."

"Golly, Eliza, your brother is something. How old is he?"

"Fourteen."

"Is he always so suave? Where does he go to school?"

"I don't know what 'suave' means, Catherine. He's a senior at Bellevue Junior High."

"'Suave' means 'sophisticated'. Is Bellevue a public school?"

"Yes." I am thinking about my brother's being 'sophisticated'. What would Catherine think if Bill had put his pet alligator in her bed under that pale peach satin comforter? How did he know that dish was a "finger bowl"? He saved me from a terrible mistake. Wouldn't it have been gross if I had eaten from the finger bowl! Why didn't Momma tell me about finger bowls?

"Catherine, show me the secret passage again."

Chapter XXV

CHRISTMAS

"Oooooh, Gamma, will Poppa ever call that he is ready?" I shiver with excitement and the chill and dark of the house. It's six o'clock Christmas morning! Poppa has gone downstairs to turn up the thermostat, to light the fire in the living room, to turn on the tree lights and to add some water to the container around the tree so the needles won't dry out and catch fire. And, he says 'to be sure that Santa has come'. He says that every year and I haven't believed in Santa Claus since the first grade. Really before that, but Poppa said if I didn't believe, then Santa would not come. I'm not one to take that kind of chance.

"All ready!" Poppa's voice is excited, too. Momma and Gamma follow Bill and me as we bound down the stairs. Gamma and I had practiced Christmas carols to sing as we slowly descended the stairs, but I can't do that right now. "Maybe next year, Gamma?"

I have a beautiful, shiny red and white bike! And a whole coconut cake from Vieh's bakery! Bill has a portable cage to take Herman around to Scout meetings and lots of outdoor scouting equipment. Our stockings are filled with apples and oranges and Hershey kisses and peppermint canes and eight quarters in the toe.

For breakfast, I don't have to eat oatmeal and I don't have to take my cod liver oil. I feast on an orange and two pieces of coconut cake. Christmas morning takes so long to get ready for and it's over so fast.

"Sally, what did you get? I got a bicycle!"

"I did, too. And a pair of jodhpurs, so I can go riding with my daddy."

"Gamma made new clothes for my Princess Elizabeth and Margaret Rose dolls. Two skirts each and Momma knitted them sweaters to match. And, Sally, I love the pen and pencil set with my name on it! Were you already going to give me that when I wanted to get it for Bill?"

"Of course! And I love my white angora mittens! They are beautiful and so soft! What about at your house?"

"Everybody loved everything! Poppa is sitting in his chair, listening to the radio and reading the paper with his new silk muffler wrapped around his neck!"

"And the holidays have just begun really. This is Monday and Wednesday is our picture show party. Lucille said she would bake some brownies for that day. We can meet here before the show and come to your house afterward. Will your tree still be up?"

"Yes, I think so. We water it everyday. And Minerva said she would make some toll house cookies for the party. Isn't everything wonderful? Can everybody in the class come? Except Catherine, I mean. I know she is going to Florida to see her grandmother."

"I think so. Isn't that fun?"

"It is wonderful! Come over when you can and we'll go down to see Lawrence."

Momma moves the four bloom red poinsettia from the coffee table to the stand in front of the hall mirror. "I can't decide where I like them best. Isn't Poppa sweet to always remember how much I like red poinsettias?"

"In front of the mirror makes them look like eight," observes

Bill as he goes out the door with Herman in the cage.

"Don't let him catch cold and be a hoarse Herman. Bill, I really like the crystal bowl you gave me. I can keep my bracelets in it on my dresser."

"And you can remember the -F.-B. dining-in," he adds with a grin.

"The president sends a message of a Merry Happy Christmas and thanks God for the United States and for peace," says Gamma as she comes from upstairs. "And we have so much to be thankful for. A prosperous and a joyous city ... needy stockings are filled and people attend church and sit down to a fine meal. Did you see in the paper where there is a gigantic, lighted Christmas tree in Union Station? A meaningful way to greet weary travelers."

"Gamma, I saw a story a few days ago. Did you see it? About the two-week old baby wrapped in newspaper?" I ask.

"I did see it. Heartbreaking and heartwarming at the same time, wasn't it? Can you imagine the despair of the mother to give up her wee one ... for fear of Stalin's bombs? And then to thrust the infant into the arms of a seven year old girl boarding a ship, trying to escape from war-torn Finland, pleading with her to guard the baby with her life."

"And they arrived in Sweden safe and sound and the doctors were amazed that the baby would live. And the seven year old girl ...."

"The good Samaritan ...."

"Yes, Gamma, she was, wasn't she? Well, she was immediately adopted into a well-to-do Swedish family. It's like a fairy story."

"That is a good story to have at Christmas time. Also that the war is quiet for today. The radio said that the allied troops frolic behind the Maginot Line and that enemies were staying apart."

"If the soldiers can agree not to shoot at each other for one day, why can't it be two days, then three, and then a week?" I ask.

Chapter XVI

NEW DECADE

"How can we stay awake until the New Year?" Lawrence asks Sally and me as we click off my birthday radio from Lux Radio Theatre.

"I don't think we'll fall asleep; we can play Monopoly as long as we want to ... to the end!" exclaims Sally, "But we might ask Gamma to tell us when it's ten minutes to midnight, just in case."

Before we know it, Gamma is knocking on the door and saying, "Girls, it's almost time! I've already heard the celebration from Times Square in New York City! Bells were ringing as the announcer counted down the minutes and then the seconds before the new decade was born! Of course, our the new decade is an hour later than Uncle Henry's"

At the first of the twelve strokes, we race out on the front porch and blow our paper horns and ring the bells we have collected and shout into the cold, still air "Happy New Year! Happy New Decade!"

"Do you feel different, Sally? Lawrence? Should we feel different? Shall we make New Decade's Resolutions?"

"I don't think so. I can't even keep my New Year's Resolutions," laughs Sally.

"Will New Year's Day be like Christmas Day when there was no fighting in the war? Why can't we keep that feeling we have on

Christmas?" I ask.

"Because feelings come and go," says Gamma. "But we can work on our attitudes. We can resolve to act with politeness whether we feel like it or not. Of course, that is not easy. Nothing worthwhile ever is."

"I wonder if I would have been able to do what the little "good Samaritan" from Finland did? And she is only seven! Where does courage come from? How do we know if we will have courage when we need it?"

"You are asking serious questions for this late at night," laughs Gamma. "Get some sleep so you can enjoy New Year's Day."

—⁓—

"What does the first page of the New Decade say, Poppa?"

"Come look at this, girls," Poppa holds up what looks like ten or fifteen papers. "Our usual paper is 22 pages and this one is 322! It is the centennial edition. Our newspaper is one hundred years old today! Gamma, there is even a congratulatory message from your president on the front page!"

"He is your president, too, Gardner," quips Gamma.

"Is there that much news, Poppa? Why is it so thick?"

"This edition is historical and it goes in the cedar chest to save. There are stories about our city and her citizens from the beginning. Whether it is the different churches, the political leaders, the floods or yellow fever, or medical care, or schools, or business, or farming, the history of it in Memphis is in this paper."

"Does it say anything about the war, Poppa? Will there be another peaceful day?"

"It is reported that Hitler hails victory in 1940 and the Britons predict a long and bitter war," reads Poppa.

Chapter XXVII

THE NEW YEAR, BITTER AND BORING

"We have never had such cold weather," shivers Momma as she takes suet out for the birds, "nor so many snows. I feel as though we've been shut up in the house for weeks. Oh, I don't mean to complain. We are warm and dry. Think of the men trying to navigate the Mississippi River. It is frozen solid above Memphis, and ice gorges are choking it here at our bluffs. We had a real blizzard."

"If the main streets get clear, I'll drive you to town to see *Gone With the Wind*," offers Poppa. "Gamma, you and Eliza and Bill, too, since you children are out of school."

Momma gives him a big smile and hug. I am jumping up and down. Gamma goes to get her hat and Bill says, "Are you paying, Poppa? The seats are $1.10 each."

"Those are the reserved seats at night and for the Sunday matinee, Bill. The weekday unreserved seats are 75¢. Which is bad enough! And yes, I am paying."

"Whoopee!"

"Would Nursey like to go? She has been shut up in either this house or her house out back. She hasn't even gotten to church."

"Ask her. Tell her it is my treat," calls Poppa as I hurry to find Nursey.

We pile into the still-new Studebaker and carefully weave our way to town. Poppa buys the tickets. "Minerva, we'll meet you right here when the movie is out," Poppa says. And I watch Nursey, spruced up in her flowered Sunday dress and black hat and with her black coat over her arm, climb the stairs to the colored balcony.

"Nursey rode to town with us. She is our guest. Why can't she sit with us?" I feel funny inside. I knew there was a colored entrance and special place for colored people to sit, but that shouldn't apply when someone is your guest. Nursey must have really been tired of the house. I wouldn't have wanted to get dressed up and come with my family and then be told I couldn't sit with them downstairs in the good seats, but had to go way up to the peanut gallery.

—∿∿—

"Four hours! That is a long movie, but wasn't it wonderful!"

"GWTW lived up to its billing!"

"I liked the first part best. When everything was beautiful. Before the war. I didn't like the war or afterward," I say.

"What about the scene when the doctor amputated the soldier's leg, and he kept screaming, 'Don't cut! Don't cut!' " Bill is commenting, more than asking.

"Nursey, I missed having you sit with me. Did you like Mammy?"

"Hattie McDaniel is a fine actress," answers Nursey, "Thank you, Mr. Horton, for treating me to the movie."

I can hardly wait to call Sally. "What did you think of Prissy when she was supposed to help Melanie have the baby and she said she didn't know 'nothin' about birthin' no babies'. All she knew was to put a knife under the bed to cut the pain," I ask her.

"Mother had a talk with me about where babies come from," replies Sally. "I had thought that you got them from the hospital or something. I'm not sure what I thought, but then I don't have any sisters or brothers."

"Suzanna's mother is going to have a baby, around Valentine's Day," I reveal, "Suzanna told me last week."

"Does she have a big stomach?"

"I don't know. I haven't seen her. But she should have if the baby is coming that soon."

"I didn't know having a baby hurt that much. I'm not sure I want to do that. Who did you like better, Melanie or Scarlet?"

"Melanie. She was so sweet. Who did you like better, Ashley or Rhett?"

"Ashley. He was such a gentleman."

"Did you hear Rhett say, 'Frankly, my dear, I don't give a damn'?"

"I sure did. But I'll think about that tomorrow," I laugh. "Do you suppose we'll have school tomorrow or will we have more snow?"

"This is February 12th and it is our twelfth snow of the winter," comments Momma. "I do feel guilty when I resent being confined to the house and being inactive. I read this article about night time in England and in Finland and I got a better perspective on my life."

"What did you read, Momma?"

"When night falls on England now, nothing happens--no street lamps, no lighted windows. All cities and towns in England plunge into 17th century darkness. The war has brought a reality of boredom, but also a prospect of doom. The blackouts have caused more deaths than the war! An average of about 32 a day," Momma shakes her head in disbelief and continues, "And in Finland, where the temperature often drops to 40 degrees below zero, the night is virtually endless. The only light is a kind of four-hour twilight that comes and goes between ten in the morning and two in the afternoon. The rest of the time, it is pitch black."

"The soldiers wear very heavy gloves because the ice-cold steel of the guns literally burns human flesh," Bill adds. "And the soldiers' home is a tent banked with dirt and snow or a dugout covered with fir and spruce branches and heated by a small stove. That takes courage to live like that day after day and be cold to the bone and never get warm all the while knowing you could be shot any moment. That's what you mean, don't you, Momma, about the 'reality of boredom and the prospect of doom'?" Bill's voice is slow and thoughtful.

"Shirley Lindy, my friend from Davis, told me something terrible the day we went to the picture show," I say.

"Oh, what's that?"

Shirley says the Germans are destroying Poland. For every Pole caught with a weapon, ten are executed. For every murder of a German Pole (they are called traitors by the Poles), 100 Poles are executed. And survivors are driven to the public squares to watch the executions! I wouldn't watch. I would just close my eyes."

"Closing your eyes to something doesn't change what is happening," Bill says quietly. "Your friend is Jewish, isn't she?"

"I don't know. I never thought about it. She did tell me though that all Jews have to wear bright yellow patches, made like triangles on their backs. That doesn't seem as bad to me as being beaten. Civil prisoners are given from 60 to 120 blows every few days with truncheons. I can't bear to hurt. I am afraid even when I go to the dentist."

"There are some hurts worse that physical ones," Momma comments.

"Like what, Momma?"

"Like seeing your child hurt or hungry; or like living in fear of what will happen next. Like the 'prospect of doom,' Bill. That is when it is so vital to have a faith to lean on."

"What good does that do? If your city is like a garbage dump; if people are starving; if typhoid is raging; if the priests are not allowed to see those condemned to die, then where is God? What has faith to do with it? If you had faith or if you didn't have faith, the city would still be a garbage dump and be raging with typhoid," Bill's voice is angry.

Chapter XXVIII

WHAT'S GOING TO HAPPEN IN MARCH?

"Now, my dear and my darlings, I am going to pose a question to you. Not to frighten you nor to make you superstitious, but to make you think.

In March 1936, Adolph Hitler seized the Rhineland;

in March 1938, he occupied and annexed Austria;

in March 1939, Hitler began the campaign to incorporate the German-speaking provinces of Czechoslovakia.

What can we look for or hope for in March 1940?"

"The bad weather will be over. My grandmother says that spring is just around the corner," I say as I raise my hand.

"We know that spring will come and the wisteria will bloom in heavy scent and purple blossom on the trellis over the driveway and that we will stop and gaze and sniff as we go across to the lunch room. Yes, that is something we know."

"And," I continue, "Poppa says Mr. Roosevelt will announce whether he will run for a third term."

"Right. Or he may tell us that by just not withdrawing his name from the presidential primaries."

"We'll have elections for the special princess to the Children's Ball," announces Margaret, standing up and looking around the class and smiling and nodding. "She is supposed to be a fifth grader." She sits down and smoothes her brown wool skirt and looks around again as if to say, 'Hey, look at me'.

"The every-ten-year census will be taken," observes Catherine. "And if a person refuses to answer any of the questions, he can be put in jail and fined $100.00. On the other hand, if a census taker tattles, he will be punished."

"The snow will melt and the earth will turn to mud and the French soldiers on sentry duty will be knee deep in mud. Momma told me that," says Renee.

"You have made some nice observations, my dears. I notice that no one mentioned Hitler's propensity for action in the month of March," Mrs. Freeland guides our discussion.

"It seems as though there hasn't been much war except in Finland and that's with Russia. Maybe Hitler will want peace," says Catherine, "but my father would call that wishful thinking."

"I think he is afraid to attack France, because the French soldiers are the best. They are unbeatable on their own ground and the Maginot Line could stop any kind of attack," Renee says with pride. "You all know about the Maginot Line?"

There are murmurs of 'yes'. "Show us on the map, Renee, where the Maginot Line is," directs Mrs. Freeland.

Renee points to the boundary of Germany and France.

"The Maginot Line does not go the whole distance, Renee. The most southern boundary, up to the Ardennes, is the most solid part of the line," explains Mrs. Freeland. "The French believe that the Ardennes Forest is so dense that an attack could not be made through it, and north of that the French share the border with Belgium. Belgium is a friendly country and France decided not to build the Maginot Line there because she reasoned that Belgium might take offense and think that France would not come to her aid if she were attacked," Mrs. Freeland explains.

"I don't know what Hitler is going to do in March, but we still have the Atlantic Ocean between us and him and nothing is going to change that," says Margaret, "And," smirking and looking around again, "We do have elections for the Children's Ball!"

"That we do," smiles Mrs. Freeland. "There will be nominations from the floor of the middle school assembly. The election will be by written ballot, with all the middle school and the middle school faculty voting. And that will be on Friday, March 15, the Ides of March. Class dismissed."

"I wonder who will be elected as special prince and princess from Davis," I say to Sally as we walk home from school. "There are two sections of the fifth grade."

"Maybe the girl comes from one section and the boy from the other. We haven't seen Bobby or Hugh or Tommy all year. I guess they've forgotten us by now."

"Where does Miss Meriwether's get the prince?"

"I think from Robertson Academy. A couple of boys from our Sunday School class go there to school. The redhead, Rob, and John Dykes."

"Who do think will be nominated?"

"Suzanna. I think she's the smartest and the class leader. She should be the princess."

"I guess one of the girls who has been there since kindergarten," Sally says. "We won't be nominated, well, for one thing we are the 'new girls'. And who would nominate us?"

"Sally, I've got it! Why don't I nominate you and you nominate me? We won't be elected but that way we can both be nominated and 'it's always an honor to be nominated,' as Momma says."

"Let's do," agrees Sally.

Chapter XXIX

ELECTIONS

"Attention, young ladies." Miss Meriwether stands tall and quiet and gently taps the little ivory bell she holds in her veined, shaky hands. "The results of balloting for our representative to the Children's Ball are complete. You know this is an important choice because the young lady will represent us at the citywide Children's Ball. Every school has a young man and a young lady representative. Of course, we pair with Robertson Academy. Our representative will reflect all the qualities of good manners, cooperation, enthusiastic participation, and kindness to the other representatives and to the adults in charge. There will be rehearsals and costume fittings. Our representative will be punctual and responsible and learn her part in the big exhibition dance that involves hundreds of children from all the schools in the city."

There is a tension and a perfect quiet; no one is breathing.

"We have a first this year. We have a tie! And there is another first! The tie is between two young ladies who are new to the school this year. Eliza Horton and Sally Long, you have both made many friends in your first year at Miss Meriwether's. Congratulations!"

Sally and I look at each other. As Momma would say, "What on earth?"

As the clapping dies down, Miss Meriwether says, "Will you two young ladies come to the front?" She extends her hand to each of us. "However, we cannot have two young ladies; we can only have one. We will not have another ballot and pit two close friends against each other. We will choose a number. I have written a number on a piece of paper and have given it to Mrs. Freeland. I want each of you to choose a number between one and ten. You may write your choice on a piece of paper."

We each write and turn in our papers. Mrs. Freeland unfolds the three papers. "Miss Meriwether, all three numbers are the same! Everyone chose the number eight!"

Murmuring and laughter break the tension. Miss Meriwether taps her bell. "Young ladies, that coincidence did not occur to me. We must think of another way to break the tie. That will be a good assignment for everyone over the weekend. Devise a fair way to break the tie. Write your name and your suggestion on a piece of paper and hand it into the office Monday morning before school and we will proceed during the Monday assembly time."

"Sally, what are we going to do?"

"I don't know. You can be the princess. You can dance. I'm better at riding horses."

"No, you can be the princess. You are more popular with the class."

"Why did we nominate each other?"

"That's right," barks Margaret overhearing that last. "Why did you nominate each other? Everybody knows you did. You all are new. This honor should go to someone who has been here a long time." Margaret makes a squenched up face and clinches her fists at her side and is quiet for a minute. Neither Sally nor I move. First she lets her face go unsquenched and then her fists and takes a heavy breath to her toes. "The princess should be someone who understands what the honor means. And knows how to act like a Meriwether Girl."

Chapter XXX

WHO IS THE PRINCESS?

"Sally, let's go talk to Miss Meriwether."

The school secretary admits us to Miss Meriwether's rose-scented office.

"Miss Meriwether, Sally and I have thought of something."

"Yes, Eliza?"

"We think the next person should be the princess."

"Why do you think that?"

"Well, then there would be no tie. And the next person wouldn't be a new girl."

"Should the princess not be a new girl?" Miss Meriwether looks slowly at me and then at Sally. It's hard not to look at the floor.

"New girls don't know what it means to be a Meriwether Girl," I blurt out.

"What do you think being a Meriwether Girl means?" the headmistress asks.

"Someone who has been at the school a long time and knows all the traditions," I answer.

"And maybe someone whose Mother went to Miss Meriwether's," whispers Sally. "And we are new."

"Any young lady who attends Miss Meriwether's is a 'Meriwether Girl'. Hopefully, we are nurturing in our young ladies qualities that will make good citizens: honesty, loyalty, responsibility, generosity, kindness, good manners, and duty. Hopefully our girls are recognized by these qualities."

"Maybe we weren't exactly honest, because we nominated each other."

"Why was nominating each other not honest? You must have wanted to be nominated?"

"Yes, Miss Meriwether. But we did not think we would be selected."

"No. We just wanted the honor of being nominated. And now, everybody is mad at us. Nobody likes us."

"Somebody likes you two or you would not be tied as winners," observes Miss Meriwether.

Sally and I look at each other. Who voted for us then? The fifth, sixth and seventh grades and the middle school faculty all vote. "But our class is mad at us."

"The whole class?" inquires Miss Meriwether.

"I don't know. I just wish this weren't happening. I wish we had not nominated each other." Sally and I nod in agreement as we leave the office.

"I would have nominated you, if Sally hadn't," says Lawrence's big sister, Cordelia. "And Barbara would have nominated Sally, if you hadn't. We had talked it over. You two may be the new girls, but you have been friendly with everybody. You haven't acted as though you know everything and you have been very sweet to my little sister. We thought it was neat the way you had the whole class to the picture show for Christmas."

"Margaret has been at Miss Meriwether's since kindergarten. Her mother graduated from Miss Meriwether's and I think her sister was princess to the Children's Ball," comments Barbara. "Maybe she expected to be chosen or maybe she is hurt or embarrassed or jealous."

"I still wish we had not nominated ourselves."

"You didn't nominate yourself. You nominated each other. And you each got your wish. Now, just draw straws or flip a coin or cut the cards or something!"

Miss Meriwether offers us all those choices on Monday at assembly period. We decide to flip a coin. We each write on a piece of paper, heads or tails. Mrs. Freeland checks the papers to be sure we haven't chosen the same thing. Miss Meriwether flips the coin. "Heads, it is!"

Mrs. Freeland announces, "Sally chose heads. She is our new princess to the Children's Ball and Eliza, you are the stand-in princess, in case something happens that Sally cannot serve. Best wishes to you both!"

"Sally, I'm glad that's over. And I'm really glad for you," I say.

"I'm glad it's you too, Sally," Margaret butts in. "Can you spend the night Friday?"

Chapter XXXI

BEING ROYALTY HAS ITS PRICE

"Drew Williams is the prince?"

"That's what Miss Meriwether said," answers Sally.

"He's Della's brother, and doesn't Mimsy like him?" I ask.

"Yes, he's Della's brother. Didn't you meet him when you spent the night with her?"

"Yes. We played a game hitting a big ball on the end of a rope and trying to make the rope wrap around the pole. I wasn't any good at it, but both Della and Drew could play. Is that how Mimsy knows Drew?" I ask.

"I think so. But I'm not sure. Anyway, he is the prince."

"And, anyway, he's cute," I giggle.

"I'm going to fit the costume today and Mamma thought you should come too, since you are the stand-in," says Sally.

"O.K. That'll be fun. It's good that we're about the same size. Do you know what the costume looks like?"

"The Cotton Carnival is all on the *Gone with the Wind* theme. The children's princesses wear white dresses that have a hoop skirt and ruffled white pantaloons that show beneath the skirt and they carry a white ruffled parasol. And the boys wear white pants and shirt and have a blue sash tied around their waists and epaulets on their shoulders. All wear white Sunday shoes," Sally sounds as though she is reading the instructions.

"When is the ball?"

"Let's see. The Royal Barge with the King and Queen of the Carnival and all the adult royalty arrives at the river bluff on Tuesday, May 14. There is other carnival stuff on Wednesday and Thursday. And then The Children's Ball is Friday afternoon, May 17. That's fifty, no fifty-two days from now; no, to be exact that is 52 and a half days from now."

"Seems like counting the days until Christmas or our birthdays! I'm glad we have birthdays in the summer. Then we don't get birthday spankings at school."

"Miss Meriwether doesn't allow birthday spankings," Sally reminds me.

"That's right, she doesn't. And I'm glad. You know, Sally, I think it's funny about time and days and counting the days. Remember Mrs. Freeland told us that the war between Russia and Finland had lasted 105 days?"

"Yes."

"Well, it's just that days and time are funny to me. I dread going to the dentist. And that thirty minutes in the dentist's chair seems forever. But thirty minutes at the picture show is no time at all. But it is still thirty minutes by the clock. I wonder what time is like to the Finns."

"I don't know. But Miss Meriwether says we must be punctual!"

Several weeks later, we are punctual at the rehearsal. Nobody else has a stand-in. I watch the rehearsal from the balcony and see how all the parts fit together. It really is neat. And Drew is cute!

"Drew, are you the only prince with two princesses?" I laugh.

"It looks that way. But then that makes me the only one who is sure to have a princess at the ball," he says easily.

He really is cute. No wonder Mimsy likes him. Maybe I'll ask Della to spend the night this Friday night.

"Sally, don't you think Drew is cute?"

"Yes. But not as cute as Rob-with-the-red-hair. I'm not going to miss Sunday School this week. Did you see Hugh is the prince from Davis?"

"Yes, I did. I've invited Della to spend the night Friday and she's coming. Maybe I can find out if Drew likes Mimsy."

Another week and another rehearsal. I can't wait to see Drew. Della has said that Drew said he liked both his princesses!

It's May the first! Carnival month and the last month of school. The whole school year is almost over. And it's nothing but fun from now on. Everything is green and beautiful outside and the windows are open. Poppa says we mustn't blare our radios or the noise will disturb the neighbors. And Memphis has a drive-in theatre! You can stay in your car and watch the picture show on a giant screen. You can put the speaker on the edge of your window and hear.

The phone rings. "I'll get it. Hello."

"Eliza, this is Sally,"

"I know. Hey."

"Guess what's happened?"

"What?"

"Grandmother telephoned ... long distance from New Orleans!"

"Wow! Is something the matter?"

"No, it's exciting! My first cousin, Diana, is getting married and I am to be the bridesmaid. Remember she's the one who was Queen of Twelfth Night in Mardi Gras last year? And we all went down for the balls and parades? I even got out of school for it!"

"I remember. You showed me the pictures."

"Well, her fiancée is a West Point graduate and the way the war looks, he and Diana thought they would not wait. The wedding is to be Saturday, May 18! At West Point! Her sister, Grace, who is married, is to be the matron of honor and her little sister, Musette and I are to be the only bridesmaids."

"That's super! Are you going? Will you have to take an airplane? Because the Children's Ball is Friday afternoon." I ask.

"I know. Mama says I have to make a choice. The whole family is taking the Thursday night train. There's a fitting for the dresses on Friday morning and a rehearsal and a dinner Friday night. And the wedding's at noon on Saturday. Diana and Richard will walk through the crossed swords after they are married!"

"Like in the movies! What are you going to do?"

"I don't know. Mama says I have to decide. I can stay here and Lucille will stay with me. Maybe y'all can give me a ride to the Ball."

"You know we will."

"But I don't really know what I want to do. One minute I want to stay and be the princess here and the other, I want to be with my family. It is very hard to decide," sighs Sally. "And Mamma says for me to choose, but I don't think she really means it. I think she's hoping I'll chose to be Diana's bridesmaid."

"Momma often says for me to choose, too. Like the time we went shopping for my new bathrobe. I wanted the silky quilted one, but she said the pink corduroy one cost less and would be easier to keep. But for me to choose which one I wanted. There was no way I could choose the one I really wanted. Then, she praised me for taking the corduroy one and making such a wise choice. But it wasn't my choice. Oh, I guess it was, because I chose to please Momma," I reason and then sigh. "Parents try to use psychology on us. It makes me mad. I want to say, 'I know what you are doing.' But I don't."

"I know. But I'll try to decide tonight and let you know when we walk to school in the morning," and Sally says goodbye.

—⁓—

"Young ladies," Miss Meriwether calls us to order with a tap of her ivory bell. "Just the way it happens in the movies sometimes, the stand-in gets to play the part. Sally has a family duty and must relinquish her crown. Eliza will represent us at the Children's Ball Friday next."

"I'm so glad that Sally had me go with her to costume fittings and to rehearsals," I respond. "So, I do know what to do. And I'll try to do my best."

"I bet she'll try to do her best to get Drew to like her." I hear this loud whisper as I return to my desk. "I'll fix her."

Why did we ever nominate each other? Except then I wouldn't have known how cute Drew is and I think he does like me. Oh, I've got to call him and tell him what has happened. 'Nice girls don't call boys on the phone,' Momma says. I'll just wait for our last rehearsal when I show up by myself. Will he be glad? Maybe Della will tell him?

I lift up my desk top to get my books for the next class. What's this red book in my desk? The Slam Book? How did that get there? Miss Meriwether doesn't allow slam books. Does anybody see? I push it to the back of my desk. Class bell is ringing. I'll do something about the book later. But what'll I do?

—⁓—

"You have a big load of books, Eliza. What are you taking home?" Margaret starts to paw through the books in my arms.

I clutch the stack to me. "The same that you have, Margaret." And I walk toward the front door.

"I bet you've got the Slam Book." She turns in the direction of the office door and shouts, "I bet Eliza Horton has the Slam Book! If she is caught with the Slam Book, she certainly shouldn't be the princess!"

———

"Sally, someone put the Slam Book in my desk. What am I going to do?" I whisper even though nobody is near us on the walk home.

"Oh, no! Have you looked at it?"

"No. Should I have?"

"I don't know. I've never seen it. I just know Miss Meriwether will punish anyone caught with one," shudders Sally. "Come on to my house. I don't have a brother to snoop."

We sit on the floor in the corner behind the bed where we can't be seen even if someone opens the door.

"Open it. Let's see it," instructs Sally.

A classmate's name is at the top of each page and on the page are written comments. Like 'Friendly', 'Sweet', 'Smart', 'Nosey'.

"Sally, are you thinking what I'm thinking? We should look for our names?"

"Yup."

"Here's your page. SALLY. 'Cute' 'Sincere' 'Good friend' 'Good to have around' 'Acts like a Meriwether Girl'. That's o.k. I don't see why Miss Meriwether forbids Slam Books," I say and then turn to my name. "Here, Sally, you read mine."

"ELIZA. 'Thinks she's cute, but she's not'; 'Thinks she's smart, but she's not'; 'Show off'; 'Conceited'; 'New girl in the worst way'; 'Wish she had never come to our school'. Sally stops. "Oh, Eliza. None of those are true."

My ears are hot and my heart is beating hard. Does my class think of me like that? "How many people signed, Sally?"

"I read you six."

"Are there more?"

"A few."

"Is there one that says something nice?"

Sally shakes her head.

"Are they written with the same handwriting?"

Sally shakes her head again.

Chapter XXXI

MAY HAS TWO FACES

"Hitler closes his stranglehold on south Norway as the Allies flee. He may hurl a blow at Sweden next," Poppa is half reading from the paper and half talking out loud.

"Poppa, do you know the Children's Ball is two weeks from today?" I wish I could tell him about the Slam Book.

Poppa puts his paper down. "Two weeks from today? My, my. You know what you will be doing two weeks from today, but I wonder about Europe."

"Are things bad, Poppa? The Maginot Line is invincible though, isn't it?"

"So some say," sighs Poppa, "We'll see, but meantime, you enjoy your Children's Ball. I do see a lot about the Carnival festivities in the paper."

The first week passes slowly. Mrs. Freeland has brought the newspaper from her home and reads from the headlines:

HITLER HURLS BLITZKRIEG BLOW AT HOLLAND, BELGIUM, LUXEMBOURG TO START 'FULL WAR'; FRENCH RUSH TROOPS; BRITISH PROMISE AID.

"Let me read a little more of this front page article," says Mrs. Freeland.

> At dawn Friday, without warning, with lightning air and land
> attacks ... the dreaded Nazi Air Force descended in swarms
> on dozens of cities, bombed airdromes and landed 100's of
> parachute troops, heavily armed with automatic weapons.
> Holland formally declares war on Germany and pledges never
> to enter negotiations with the enemy.

Mrs. Freeland sighs and says, "I do not believe there is a place in God's world that is not beautiful in May. Even in Morocco, the brown hills are green and poppies and calla lilies and hibiscus and bougainvillea all bloom red and white and yellow and magenta. How can the world be bloody and cruel in the midst of such evidence of God's abundant love?"

"We still have the oceans between us, Mrs. Freeland. And no army can break the Maginot Line."

"And May is beautiful here and the Carnival is next week."

"And then school is out!"

"That's right, my dears and my darlings. But when you say your prayers, remember especially the Dutch and Belgian children who are your age and try to imagine what they are feeling and pray for them and their families."

I say my prayers at night. Always. And I pray for those children and for Princess Elizabeth and Margaret Rose. But it is hard to imagine what they are feeling. Have all the fathers gone to the army or navy? Have they been wounded? Does the family have enough to eat? What is it like when the planes appear out of the sky and drop bombs and paratroopers? What if a bomb were to hit our house? It would explode and burn. Would we escape? Where would we escape to? And if things were that bad, I wouldn't care about the Slam Book. And maybe I would do something brave and save somebody's life and then they would write under my name 'courageous' and 'modest'. And I wouldn't have to figure out how to get rid of the yukky red book.

Saturday's headlines are better:

ALLIES STEM NAZI SMASH WITH FIRE AND FLOOD.

I knew it! We will win ... or rather the good French and good English will win and the bad Nazi's will get what's coming to them and we don't need to worry. And the Royal Barge arrives on Tuesday night!

Fireworks over the river! And music and bands and hundreds of people in beautiful costumes and the King and Queen in glittering crowns and mantles. And it doesn't rain! Best of all, Drew and his parents and Della take Sally and me to see it. Oh joy!

"Poppa, are there pictures of the barge and the fireworks in this morning's paper?" I ask over my oatmeal.

"I think so," and Poppa hands me the second section.

"Isn't the arrival of the barge on the front page?" I ask.

"So, it is," answers Poppa and hands me the first section.

"That's just how it looked, Poppa. Except, of course, the fireworks were full of color." My eyes wander from the left side of the front page to the right. **NAZIS FORCE DUTCH TO SURRENDER!**

"Oh, Poppa! But the Maginot Line? It will stop the Nazis?"

"I hope so."

I go by Sally's after school that afternoon. She is packing and leaves tomorrow for the wedding. Her dress is a lovely yellow and she'll carry a bouquet of white and yellow daisies and will wear some daisies in her hair. She's glad she chose to go to the wedding. We'll decide what to do about the Slam Book when she gets back. The afternoon paper lies unopened on her father's footstool.

"I'm not allowed to touch Daddy's paper until he's seen it," Sally says to me as she sees me looking at it.

"I'm not unfolding it. I just want to peep at the headlines," I say.

"I don't know. I'm not supposed to touch it."

"O.K., I'll look at ours when I get home."

"Well, bye. Have a good time at the Children's Ball, and with Drew," Sally giggles.

"You have a good time being in the wedding and call me when you get home and tell me all about it. Bye."

It takes me ten minutes to walk home from Sally's house. There's that time thing again. I want to hurry home and see what is in the papers, but I also want to think about the Children's Ball and Drew's holding my hand. Just thinking about that makes me tingle.

I open the paper. **GERMANS CLAIM THE MAGINOT LINE IS PIERCED!** I don't believe that. That's just what the Germans claim. That's just their scare propaganda. It will all be clear in the morning ... Friday morning. The day of the Children's Ball!

Chapter XXXIII

SCHOOL IS OUT

FDR TELLS CONGRESS: U.S. IN PERIL; ARM NOW!
But the headlines don't say anything about the Maginot Line! I knew that was propaganda. Now I can concentrate on Drew and the ball!

Hundreds of girls in white hoop dresses and pantaloons and parasols and hundreds of boys in white slacks with blue sashes are glorious! I'm nervous that I will make a mis-step and mess up the pattern of the dance. But I guess everybody is. The colored lights wave and swirl and the music is magic. We do the dance perfectly and Drew holds my hand, long after he has to! The finale is followed by everyone's standing and belting out "Dixie"! My eyes are full of tears, but I am so happy! This is the most wonderful day of my life! How can the world be so happy?

"Eliza, it's Sally on the phone," calls Momma.

"Hey. How was the wedding?"

"Super! I'm so glad I went. It was soooooo romantic! The cadets in their uniforms are soooooo handsome. Richard and Diana looked like movie stars! And they are sooooo in love!"

"How you know when you're in love? Do you know, Sally?"

"Well, not really, but they gaze into each other's eyes and hold hands a lot."

"Oh, they do?"

"And I'm sure they kiss a lot, like in the movies. But when they are by themselves. They kissed after the the minister said, "I now pronounce you man and wife" and after they came through the swords. I imagine she nearly melts when they kiss."

"I guess she feels all tingly. The way I feel when Drew holds my hand. I can't imagine what I would feel if he were to kiss me ... on the cheek, I mean."

"How was the ball?"

"It was like a dream! And at the end everybody sang "Dixie" and clapped to the music!"

"Well, we've got exams next week, then our class outing, then moving-up day and then we are out for three months of no school work," exclaims Sally.

"Except for Catherine," I say.

"What do you mean?"

"Catherine failed arithmetic and has to go to summer school. Every morning for six weeks."

"I think arithmetic is hard," confesses Sally.

"But you didn't fail," I add.

"Catherine's smart. How can she have failed? We haven't had our exams yet. Are her grades that low?" asks Sally.

"I'm not sure. That's just what she told me."

"Why don't we help her? We've got every afternoon this week and Saturday and Sunday. I bet if she worked real hard she could pass the exam."

"Sally, that's a great idea. Surely Miss Meriwether wouldn't fail her if she passed the exam. We could have a study hall every afternoon. And just start at the beginning of the book and work through it," I say.

"And your mother could help us. Didn't she used to teach math?"

"Right! I'll ask Momma and then call Catherine and see if she wants to. Bye."

We work every afternoon: on the multiplication tables and the division tables and fractions and percentages. Catherine gets permission to walk to school with us and we drill all the way there and all the way home. Then Momma helps us with word problems.

"I hope the rest of your studies will not suffer because of all the time you are devoting to arithmetic. Are you also drilling on your vocabulary words? And your French verbs?" worries Momma.

"Yes, Mrs. Horton, we don't talk or even think about anything but school work. And for Eliza, that is something," Sally looks at me and mouths "Drew."

In a whirl, exams are over. Catherine passes! Her arithmetic teacher says, "I knew you could do it. You just did not apply yourself until the last week."

Catherine's mother invites Sally and me over for tea in the air-conditioned summer house at the back of the garden. We've never been anywhere that was air-conditioned except the picture show downtown. It feels really cold when you first walk in the summer house and then, Catherine says 'You get used to it and it doesn't feel so cool.' We have tea in thin china cups and little cucumber sandwiches and scones with jam!

"I'm certain Catherine will keep up with her daily work and not have this scare again. Is that correct, Catherine?" asks her mother.

"Yes, Mother." After a while, Mrs. Hunt returns to her garden.

"Catherine, show Sally the secret passage," I whisper.

Sally's eyes widen. "Let's get a flashlight and see what we can discover. Maybe it leads to the river, like in *Catherine and Essex*!"

"Father does not wish us to play in the secret passage. But he's away on business and Mother's in the garden and Mrs. Muzzy-dear has the afternoon off to visit her niece," Catherine is thinking through Sally's request.

"Catherine, please. I have always wanted to explore the secret passage," I beg.

"Well, you all have helped me not to have to go to summer school, I guess I could at least let you see the passage," Catherine agrees. "But I don't have a flashlight and if I ask James for one, he'll suspect we are up to something."

"We could each take a candle," suggests Sally.

"There are candles in the dining room and there are matches in the guest room," I add.

The panel squeaks a bit as we push it open and squeeze through. Our hands are shaking as we strike the matches. There is a small circular staircase, going straight up. We each clutch a lighted candle and tiptoe up. There is not much room at the top of the circular stairs, just a wall.

"You push here," instructs Catherine as she bends down and pushes at the bottom of the wall. And it swings open! And we are behind heavy draperies in the upstairs hall. "See, this way you can come upstairs without being seen."

"But then where would you go? Or would you just hide behind the draperies until the coast is clear?"

"You could, because there is a niche in the wall and you would not make the draperies bulge," Catherine speaks as though she has done this before. "There are other passages," she dares to say.

"Where? Show us," Sally and I speak as one.

"This way," and Catherine leads us into her father's suite. "See, where the logs are piled beside the fireplace?"

"Yes."

"Well, those are make-believe logs attached to the panel door that swings open when you wiggle the smallest log on the bottom row!"

"Well, I never! This is better than the movies!" I exclaim.

"Can we try it?" asks Sally. "I would like to see what's back there. Where does it go?"

"We've come this far. We can't get in any more trouble," reconciles Catherine and wiggles the smallest log. The panel swings out and we duck inside with our still-lighted candles and pull the panel closed. There is another circular stair. We slowly and carefully make our way down. Again we are met with a blank wall. "Push at the top right," instructs Catherine.

We do and the door swings out! We step out into the drawing room right beside the fireplace. We close the panel, which looks just like the panel on the other side of the fireplace.

"Wait! I hear voices. Quick, blow out your candle. Go sit at the piano and start to play," Catherine says quickly.

"I can't play," I confess. "Neither can Sally."

Catherine quickly slides on the bench and starts her scales as Mrs. Hunt comes in.

"Catherine, I smell something burning. Do you smell it?"

"No, Mother," answers Catherine scarcely looking up from her practicing.

"I will check with James. It was nice to have you at tea, Eliza and Sally. Do come again."

Sally and I both stand up and say, "Thank you, Mrs. Hunt; we will."

"Catherine, do you think I'm conceited?" I blurt out.

"No. That's a funny question. Not funny 'Ha, Ha' but funny 'peculiar,'" answers Catherine. "Look how you and Sally helped me. That's not conceited."

We tell Catherine about the Slam Book.

"Where is the book? Is it at school? It better not be at school," warns Catherine. "They clean the desks at the end of the year."

"No. It's at my house now. Hidden," I confess. "I would burn it, but Momma would think something was up. A fire in the summer? I thought about tearing out the pages and flushing them down the toilet. But that might stop up the toilet and Momma might have to call the plumber and ...."

"You say all those bad things were written in different hand writing? Are you sure? Could they have been written by one person who tried to disguise her writing?" Catherine questions.

Chapter XXXIV

THE IMPOSSIBLE HAPPENS

"This has been the most fateful week in the memory of living men," reads Poppa from this week's *Life*. "The German Army, rolling down on Paris, wheeled suddenly west across the Plain of Flanders, caught a huge Allied Army in its trap and swept on to the English Channel."

"How is that happening? Are the Nazis supermen, the way they claim?" I want to be reassured.

"No, Eliza, the Germans are not supermen. As this article points out, seven years ago they were the bitterest, most frustrated people in Europe. Then from the dregs, rose a man with an Idea that galvanized a desperate nation. Now he threatens to conquer an entire continent."

"How can they beat good people?"

"The German Army has superb organization. Oil trucks keep right behind the tanks to provide the necessary fuel. When their bombers blast and destroy a bridge, the engineers are right behind, throwing up a new bridge amid the smoking ruins of the old one," Poppa explains. "And you have learned a new word *Blitzkreig*?"

"Yes, Poppa, I know that means 'a lightning war'. But I'm not really sure what that means."

" 'Lightning war' is correct because the strike moves with the speed and suddenness of lightning. Also, there is the combination of tanks and bombing planes. Some of the tanks can throw flames. The German Army is equipped for mass killing."

"The cover picture of this issue is in color. The Statue of Liberty against a blue, blue sky. That looks so safe and strong. But inside are pictures of hundreds of refugees stumbling down dusty roads and of starving people in Warsaw cutting up a dead horse," I bemoan. "I want this summer to be wonderful, like last summer."

On Monday, June 10th the headlines read:

ITALY DECLARES WAR!
DUCE'S ARMIES INVADE FRANCE

Mussolini announced from a Venice balcony to a wildly cheering crowd: 'We are going to war against the decrepit democracies to break the chains that tie us in the Mediterranean. There is but one word for Fascists. It is to win!'

"What does this mean, Poppa? What is Duce? What is Fascist?"

"D-u-c-e" is pronounced 'doo-chay' and it is from an Italian term 'il duce,' meaning 'the leader.' Benito Mussolini has taken it as his title. Now 'Duce' also means 'dictator.'" Poppa answers the first question.

"And 'fascist'?"

"A 'fascist' is one who advocates or follows 'Fascism.' That doesn't tell you much, does it?" chuckles Poppa.

"No. You know you don't allow us to give a definition that way," I try to smile at Poppa's joke. I wish I could tell him about the Slam Book.

"'Fascism' is a program, or government, if you will, that exercises severe national control over industry, commerce, and finance. There is strict censorship and heavy repression of anyone who disagrees. It is hard for you to understand because our country does not exercise severe governmental control over industry, commerce or finance. Although, I will have to say that President Roosevelt has taken some powers into his hands that seem out of line to me," answers Poppa.

"But we don't have censorship. Right, Poppa? You can speak out against the president if you want to?"

"Right, and I do when I think it is the thing to do. Say, isn't this your summer vacation? Don't you and Sally have some fun cooked up?" The phone rings as Poppa says this.

"Hey, Sally. I knew it was you."

"Let's plan an all-day swim at Clearpool. You know, four mothers to play cards in the shade and we can swim and eat lunch and Hugh is a junior life guard at Clearpool this summer!"

Sally is scheming, I can tell. "Let's do. How about Lawrence and her mother? And maybe, Della and her mother? Do you think Drew might come?" This scheme sounds better and better. "Why don't you spend the night tonight? I'll ask Momma if you can come and you can ask your mother if you can come if I ask you."

"O.K. Bye."

The whole neighborhood plays out until after dark while Gamma swings on the front porch glider. Then we catch fireflies in a big jar. We have at least a hundred blinking lights. "Shall we let them go now?" I ask.

"No," says Bill, "I need them."

"You are not going to feed these beautiful creatures to Herman," I cry.

"No, Herman only likes plain household flies. Lightning bugs give him heartburn," answers Bill.

"What are you going to do with them?" I demand.

"Aren't you going to the picture show tomorrow?" he asks Sally and me.

"Yes, Margaret asked Sally and Sally said she was doing something with me, so she asked me too. I think Mimsy and Renee are going. Renee is very upset because the Nazis are so close to Paris. Her uncle still lives there."

"Is Catherine going?" asks Bill.

"I don't think so," I reply.

"Why don't you ask her? I might even go with you."

"You are up to something. You don't like to go the picture show with us," I observe.

"I thought I might let the fireflies loose in the theatre!" Bill is known for his original thoughts.

"Super!!" we all say at once. "How are you going to smuggle in this big jar?"

"You'll see. Only The Shadow Knows!!!"

Early Friday morning the phone rings. "Yes, Renee, what is it? I cannot understand you. Say it again slowly," Momma tries to calm her own voice. "Of course, I will tell her and I know she and Sally will want to see you. Goodbye."

"Renee says the Germans have occupied Paris. She was weeping. Where is the paper? Bill, turn on the radio."

"That's what the headlines say, Momma: **NAZIS ENTER PARIS ABANDONED BY THE FRENCH ARMY.** Then in smaller letters: *French move their capital to Bordeaux.* Oh,no! Does this mean the war is lost?"

"Let me see," says Bill. "No, it says that this is the sixth time in history that Paris has fallen and this does not decide the war."

"Maybe Renee didn't read that far. Should I call and tell her?"

"The best thing would be for you and Sally to go over to see Renee. I will be glad to drive you," offers Momma.

"Do you think she will still want to go to the movie with us this afternoon?" I am remembering the fireflies.

"She may and she may not. You can ask her."

Renee goes with us to the picture show and Bill lets the hundred fireflies loose. They look like twinkling stars! We think it is super and so daring. Since most of the audience is made up of children, there is lots of laughter. Except from the ushers. But then they are paid to be serious. Renee forgets her sadness and laughs too. All too soon *Pinocchio* is over and we are back to our real world.

Sunday's paper says: "Swastika flies on Eiffel Tower in a Paris like City of Dead."

"Yes," says Poppa, "the Nazi war flag flies over Vienna, Prague, Danzig, Warsaw, Copenhagen, Oslo, the Hague, Brussels and Paris. Only nine months and 14 days after the declaration of war."

The week goes slowly. We spend a lot of time with Renee. Next Sunday's headlines say: **TEARFUL FRENCH EMISSARIES ACCEPT 'HARD BUT HONORABLE' HITLER PEACE.**

"How can a Hitler-peace be a peace?" I ask. "What happened to the Maginot Line?"

Chapter XXXV

THE SUMMER OF 1940

"The picture show now costs more," I explain to Poppa, "so I need an increase in my allowance."

"How much more?" asks Poppa. "Before you answer that, can you tell me why there is now a tax on theatre admissions?"

"I'm not sure, Poppa."

"Our country has to raise more money to cover the new defense programs."

"Like building planes and ships?" I ask.

"Yes. And ammunition. For example, a powder plant is to be built right here in Shelby County, which, incidentally, will create 10,000 jobs for our area. But we need more than planes, ships, and ammuntion. We need people. Planes alone do not make an air army. For every plane, there must be ten men to service it, in addition to the pilot. And an air army cannot save a country unless it is backed by a land army," continues Poppa.

"And a land army needs clothes and shoes," adds Momma. "President Roosevelt was saying all that when he asked for Congress to give him the authority to call the National Guard into service. I am thankful that Bill is not quite yet 15. Surely this will all be over before he is finished high school."

"Eliza, I could give you the few cents extra to cover the tax on theatre admissions, but who is going to give me the extra to cover all the other taxes that I am certain to have to pay?" asks Poppa. "I think perhaps we shall just all try to live within what we have."

"Anyway, you'll probably have to skip a movie or two and swimming too," observes Bill, "because surely there'll be a case of infantile paralysis and Momma won't let us be in crowds."

"I hope not. Polio is so scary," I say. "I wish we were in Rhode Island. I don't remember hearing anything about polio there."

"No. But you heard plenty about the war and that was a year ago before Hitler had even invaded Poland. And they don't have a picture show, remember? You can live without one," Bill is half-teasing and half-serious.

"Here comes the postman," says Gamma as she opens the front door to take the mail from him. "Good afternoon," says Gamma, "did you bring me the letter I was watching for this morning?"

"I think so, Mrs. Milton. There is a letter from Rhode Island. Your brother?" asks the postman.

Gamma smiles her thanks and gets her letter opener. "It is from Henry. He has news! He is getting married!"

"What? You don't mean it?"

"Is he marrying Aunt Lucy?"

"When?"

"Wait. Let me read the whole letter. He is marrying a friend of Julia's, whose name is Amy. She is a maiden lady."

"What about Aunt Lucy?" I cry. "Aunt Lucy loves Uncle Henry."

"Uncle Henry must not love her," Bill hits the nail on the head.

"We must be happy for Uncle Henry. Now he won't be so lonely," Gamma says calmly.

"But Aunt Lucy will be lonelier," I am on the verge of tears, "lonelier than ever."

"Shall we hear the rest of the letter?" asks Gamma.

"Yes. When is the wedding to be?" says Momma.

"Saturday, August 17, at four in the afternoon at St. Andrew's-by-the-Sea and a reception afterward on the back lawn of Mallow Marvel," reads Gamma, "and he wants us to come! What do you think of that?"

"I think that's cool," responds Bill.

"I can see Frances and Anna and Caroline and Elizabeth and find out more about the mysterious blue rings and maybe see where the eighth step was tampered with. And best of all, I can play 'Sympathy' with Aunt Lucy." Maybe, I think to myself, I will tell her about the Slam Book. Better still, I could take it in my suitcase and burn it in the grate on a cool night! "Momma, can we go?"

"May we go?" corrects Momma. "Honey, what do you think?"

"I see no reason for Bill and Eliza not to go for this special event. Uncle Henry is kind to want them. You both must have behaved yourselves last summer?" Poppa looks as Bill and then at Gamma, "Gamma, are you willing to have the responsibility again?"

"Of course, Gardner. Eliza and Bill are now experienced train-travelers and can look after me," smiles Gamma.

"And it will be an extra bonus to get the children out of the city during these hottest months." adds Momma.

I know she's thinking about polio. If I even look funny, she pushes my chin to my chest and says, "Does that hurt?"

"When will we leave?" asks practical Bill.

"After my birthday, I hope. Sally has asked me to spend the day and night with her on the day before my birthday. A surprise day, she says.

"I guess you want fried chicken for your birthday dinner and birthday cake and ice cream," muses Momma. "Or did you want a little afternoon birthday party?"

"Momma, that would be fun. How many could I have?"

"Just let me know when it's going to be so I can be someplace else, like the morgue," mocks Bill, "all those little girls giggling."

"Now, Bill, someday, you will like those 'little girls,'" reminds Momma. "Let's see, Eliza, what sort of games do you want to have?"

"We could do the memory game. You know, where you put about twenty things on a tray, like scissors, a crayon, a band aid, and everybody gets one look at the tray and then has to write down as many as she remembers. The one who remembers the most gets the prize. And we could do the camouflage game where you hide things around the house in full view but they are disguised by being the same color as their background, like pink embroidery thread on a pink bath towel," I am warming up to this.

"Really sounds thrilling," cracks Bill. "What are you going to have to refresh yourselves after such a strenuous afternoon?"

Ignoring him, I continue, "And play 'it isn't Jeanie, it's the moon." We learned it at camp last summer. I don't think anybody knows it's here. You know, 'it isn't red but it is green. It isn't your toe, it is your foot. Now, you say one."

"It isn't pink, but it's blue."

"No."

"It isn't your finger, it's your hand."

"No. But it isn't your ankle, it is your heel."

"Wait, let me try again. It isn't sweet but it's sour."

"No, again. It isn't sour, but it is sweet."

"Okay, I give up."

"No, you can't give up, you just keep listening and finally you catch on and join the ones saying it right. It's fun. Of course, we could jump rope or play hopscotch, but it is so hot. And we could go swimming, but I know that's not a good idea now. We could play Monopoly and Parcheesi."

"You know what, Eliza, since you are having that big day with Sally, and since you will be leaving shortly on this big trip, I think maybe we ought to skip a party this year and just have a family dinner. Fried chicken, of course, and ice cream and cake," Momma says.

"Momma, I don't want to ask for too much, but I didn't have my friends for a birthday party last year."

"I know. You were on a big trip and we did come up to see you," reminds Momma.

"She just wants all the presents," says Bill.

"I do not!" I hotly retort.

"It's expensive and a lot of work to get ready. Why don't you call the train and the farm your birthday party?" Bill asks.

"When September rolls around, are you going to call the trip your birthday party?" I respond.

"Sure. I don't need to play 'It isn't Jeanie, it's the moon,'" retorts brother Bill.

Chapter XXXVI

STOP THE TRAIN

"It is hard to pass the time on an all-day train ride, but I can tell you about my day with Sally and her daddy," I say to Gamma as we settle on the Pullman seats that ride with the train.

Bill looks up from his sailing book, "Did you and Sally ride bareback?"

"No, we rode an English saddle. And I learned to post. You should see Sally post. She can really do it. She looks so good in her jodhpurs. She can trot and canter. Her daddy jumps too. The country is beautiful, but it really was hot in the ring and dusty. It was much cooler on the trail, sort of through the woods."

"Did you have a picnic?" asks Gamma.

"Yes, under the trees on the grass. We had stuffed eggs and potato salad and pimento cheese sandwiches and tomato sandwiches with Lucille's homemade mayonnaise and soft white bread and mustard sandwiches and dill pickles and Lucille's brownies. It was delicious!" My mouth is watering just remembering. "Then you know, we went back to Sally's house and took off for the picture show. We saw *The Wizard of Oz*."

"Are you just now seeing that?" asks Bill.

"Of course not, we had both seen it before, but we wanted to see it again. Now we know it practically by heart. Especially 'Over the

Rainbow.' You know, 'Somewhere over the rainbow, skies are blue, and the dreams that you dare to ....'"

"Please don't sing. I have sensitive ears," says Bill.

"I sing in the Children's Choir at Sunday School," I defend myself.

"Then your choir master is deaf!" vows Bill.

"I have sung in the choir for five years. And I have never missed. Don't you remember my pins for perfect attendance?"

"Hush, children," says Gamma. "Eliza, then you spent the night with Sally after the movie? What did you do?"

"Sally has a super room. Her mother lets her put movie star pictures all over the walls. She has Deanna Durbin and Errol Flynn and John Payne. Those she cut out of movie magazines, but we wrote off to get some of Ronald Coleman.

"Wow! Whoopee!" smirks Bill.

"I am ignoring you," I say. "Anyway, Gamma, Sally has a spool bed very much like mine. Catherine and Suzanna have twin beds with little posts. We must have stayed up pretty late because Mr. Long had to come knock on the door and tell us to go to sleep. It was fun."

A smiling waiter in a white coat walks through the car hitting a chime. "It's time to dine!" he sings.

We make our way to the dining car, still an adventure but a comfortable one, knowing how to open the doors and what to look for and how to move with the jerks and lurchings of the cars. The fried chicken is just as good as last summer and ....

"Mrs. Milton," interrupts the conductor, "you are Mrs. Milton?"

"Yes, conductor, I am Mrs. Milton, what is it? You have already punched our tickets." Gamma is startled.

"I must ask you and the children to follow me. Is this Eliza?"

"What on earth is the matter? We have not finished our dinner. I do not understand," Gamma's hands are shaking.

"I am sorry to interrupt your meal. I will have the waiter package your dinners and bring them to you. Please come with me."

My heart is pounding. Bill steadies Gamma as we silently follow the conductor who leads us into a compartment.

"Please, have a seat. Mrs. Milton, I am so sorry to distress you, but we just received word by wire that Eliza's playmate, Sally Long, had been diagnosed with infantile paralysis. Eliza has been exposed. We must now quarantine her and return her to Memphis."

Chapter XXXVII

WHAT WE DREADED, HAPPENED

"Sally has infantile paralysis? I don't believe it! How can you be sure? She was fine when I talked to her Wednesday. She didn't say anything about having a stiff neck or having fever," I am talking loud and shaking my head.

"Please have a seat and take a deep breath and don't talk for a few minutes. I know this is a shock," the conductor leads Gamma and me to the seats. He turns to Bill, "You were not with Sally but you have been with your sister?"

"That is correct, sir. But really only today. Saturday. We've all been pretty busy getting our things ready for this trip," replies Bill.

"My instructions were to transfer Eliza to a train back to Memphis as soon as possible. As I understand Eliza and Sally had spent the day and the night together. Slept in the same bed." The conductor's voice sounds off in the fog somewhere.

"Is Sally bad sick? Is ...," I pause and swallow and try to get the words out, "She's not paralyzed, is she?" Tears come from nowhere and roll down my face. I sob.

Gamma enfolds me in her arms, "There now, we haven't heard what her case is. I've known of cases in which the patient is walking and running again and one cannot even tell the child ever had infantile paralysis." Gamma rocks me back and forth saying this over and over.

"Knoxville is our next stop," the conductor looks at his pocket watch. "We should be there in twenty-eight minutes. We have a compartment for you, Eliza, on the train going to Memphis. The question to me is should your brother be quarantined with you? Mrs. Milton, there is scarce risk to adults. You are free to continue on to, let's see, you are going to Providence, right? With a change of trains in NYC?"

"Let me think a minute," says Gamma as she continues to wipe my face and hug me. "I don't know about Eliza's riding alone. This is a shock to us all, but Sally is her special friend. She would be accompanied only by fearful thoughts."

"I can ride with her, Gamma," Bill says firmly. "There is a question about me anyway. And you can go on to the farm. Uncle Henry is counting on you to be his family. And Aunt Lucy needs you too."

At the mention of Aunt Lucy's name, I begin to howl, until finally I half-choke and half-hiccup in an effort to stop crying.

"I will leave you for about ten minutes so you can talk out your decisions. Mr. and Mrs. Horton will meet the train in Memphis. I am sorry to be the bearer of such upsetting news," and the conductor closes the door behind him.

"What you suggest makes sense, Bill. Uncle Henry is counting on me. And if you ride with Eliza, then I won't be as concerned about her. You all can talk." Gamma shakes her head and sighs, "We never know what a day will bring. A day is like a grab bag. We reach in and never know what we are going to bring out."

We make the transfer to the Memphis-bound train in the early dark of a summer's night. Gamma's train pulls out before ours. I cannot understand what I feel. There is Gamma going on by herself to that dear, dear Mallow Marvel Farm ... to see Uncle Henry get married! And to be there to see Aunt Lucy at the wedding. Or maybe

Aunt Lucy won't go to the wedding. I won't see the blue, blue sea or my friends or the eighth step. Or burn the Slam Book in the parlor grate. But what has happened to Sally? Are they afraid I will get polio too? I hadn't really thought about that. Is Sally in the isolation hospital? We've driven past there lots of times on our way home from church and have seen people standing on boxes so they would be tall enough to see in the window and wave at their loved ones. And wave is all they can do, because you can't talk loud enough to be heard. "Sally couldn't be in an iron lung. That's just not possible. How long do I have to stay isolated?" I ask Bill.

"I don't know. I don't know much about infantile paralysis, except that Momma has always feared it. I thought it started with high fever and a stiff neck, although a boy in my class got polio last year and his started with a sore throat and an upset stomach, sort of like flu. His family didn't think anything about it until his legs got weak. Then they called the doctor."

"How is he? Was he paralyzed?"

"He uses braces and crutches."

"Ohh," and I begin to cry again.

Momma and Poppa are at the station and hug us both quietly and hard.

"How is Sally?"

"The doctor's don't really know much. They say we have to wait and see."

"Where is she?"

"At the isolation hospital," Momma's voice quivers.

Chapter XXXVIII

"THE REALITY OF BOREDOM, THE PROSPECT OF DOOM"

"**B**ill, the doctor says that you do not have to be quarantined," explains Momma, "and for that I am glad. But you made a wise and compassionate decision to ride with your sister on the train."

"That seemed the right thing to do, Momma. I was glad to," Bill sounds so mature.

I write to Sally every day. And I call her parents every other day. She will be at the isolation hospital for six weeks and will be getting therapy. Her parents can only see her a few minutes at a time. What is she thinking, lying there all by herself, aching and hurting all over? The doctors call the hurt "spasms."

July 17, 1940

Dear Sally,
You are there in the hospital and I am here at home and we cannot either one leave where we are and we cannot even talk on the phone, so I am going to write to you just as though we were talking.

Of course, I'm real sorry not to see Aunt Lucy and everybody. And the S.B. just rode back home in my suitcase. Oh woe!

Mrs. Freeland sent the geography class a letter telling about our assignment for August! Each one of us is to follow a topic for the month of August and be ready to report on it when school starts.

Renee, of course, chose to report on France although I would think that would make her even sadder. I chose England because of Princess Elizabeth and Margaret Rose and I chose the presidential elections for you.

I'll write you what I find out so you won't be behind when school starts.

This week I am cutting out pretty rooms from Momma's magazines. Only the rooms I really like and am making pictures of my ideal house. There is an entrance hall with a spiral staircase that is elegant.

Get better every day.

Love from your friend,
Eliza

July 20, 1940

Hey Sally,

It is really funny. There was a letter to the editor in the paper which said that all war is wrong, that the only way America can guard democracy is to stay out of war and concentrate on bad housing and poverty at home.

Another letter said that America is losing time by failing to enlist men for military training. That we need the draft. We need to get ready for war.

So who is right?

The candidates for president are:
Pres. Roosevelt (Democratic Party),
Mr. Wendell Willkie (Republican Party),
Col. Charles Lindbergh (Isolationist Party).

Col. Lindbergh said he thought the Nazis would finish off the British within a month. What does he know just because he flew over the Atlantic Ocean?

Today I started a stamp collection. Poppa bought me a big sack of used stamps. I am tracing maps of Europe and South America and pasting the stamps in the proper country. It is sort of fun, but I'd rather be playing Monopoly with you.

I miss you so much. Please get well.

Love from your friend,
Eliza

July 24, 1940

Hey Sally,

I talked to your folks this morning and today makes two weeks since you got sick. The doctors don't say much. But your therapist said you are a brave and determined young lady. We know that.

I just heard about the Quiz Kids. The five brainy children on the weekly radio show. Each week a Quiz Kid is on the show he earns a $100.00 bond.

There's a seven year old who knows 300 bird songs! There is a 14 year old girl who writes words and music, who has studied German for five years, and swims and plays hockey, and figure skates and likes the movies. I'm glad we have one thing in common.

Catherine is home from Florida. She chose China for her country and said to tell you hello and that the war in China is in its fourth year. She says as soon as you are well, she will show us more of the secret passage!

Bill has been very sweet. He has not teased me with Herman since I have been quarantined.

Talked to Margaret; said she had sent you several cards and she was sorry this had happened to the two new girls. I truly don't think she was being catty. I think she meant to be nice.

With love from your friend,
Eliza

July 31, 1940

Hey Sally,
Think of all the picture show money we are saving!

Lawrence called and sent you a hug and said she
would even let you have Park Place next time we
play Monopoly!

Half-way this week! Next Wednesday, Momma
will bring me to stand on the box and wave to you.
I'll bring you the latest movie magazine. And
another surprise!

Hang on!

Much love from your friend,
Eliza

August 8, 1940

Hey Sally,
I could really see you through the window! I used to
think people were funny to stand out there on the
boxes and wave, but I don't think that anymore. I
would come every day if Momma could bring me.

Didn't you like your surprise? I wrote to Deanna
Durbin as soon as you were sick and asked her to
autograph a picture just for you. I wasn't sure that
she would, but she did! That will make you
well quicker!

I've been out of quarantine a week. I guess that means
I won't get infantile paralysis ... this time anyway.
Momma still won't let me go swimming or to the movie.

Only two more weeks!

With love from your friend,
Eliza

—∿∿—

August 15, 1940

Hey Sally,

I hope your hospital room has lots of fans. It's been
sweltering here. Momma and Poppa saw an ad about
an attic fan. They know the Smiths who had one
installed. The fan pulls the hot, stuffy air out of the
house through the attic and draws in the cool night air
through the windows. Isn't that amazing?

Mr. Smith said that since their attic fan had been
installed, they had been able to sleep soundly every
night. In fact, they had to get an alarm clock to be
sure to wake up in time in the morning.

There was some drama in the sky this week. On an
airplane coming from Chicago, a stewardess was hurt.
Some man demanded that she give him the key to the
baggage compartment. She, of course, refused. The
passengers heard him shout, "Give me the key! Give me
the key or I'll slug you!" He tried to take it from her
and she swallowed it! And then he hit her.

I wonder if she had been trained what to do? What do you think will happen to the key? Was it a sharp key with edges that would hurt her insides? If she had been trained to swallow it, it might have been a round, funny kind of key that wouldn't hurt her insides and would just come on out ... you know.

More later.

Much love from your friend,
Eliza

—⁓—

August 22, 1940

Hey Sally,
The last week! I am so excited. All your friends are. I can't even imagine what you are. Your mother and father said the doctors would know then the extent of the damage to the nerves. I thought they meant you would be well at the end of six weeks.

But you will be out of isolation and can probably go home. Right? And we all believe that your legs will be fine. We just know they will be.

I want to tell you a little about the Republican Party's nominee for President. He (Wendell Willkie) is from a small-busted town in Indiana, called Elwood. Mr. Willkie is proud of his town but says it represents the story of America and our problems. He says the time is long past when America can let any of its citizens get rich by "unchecked shoveling of its natural resources."

I cut out his picture. His hair always looks uncombed and he looks excited.

You already know about the tax on our picture show tickets and there are other taxes too. On alcoholic drinks, on cigarettes, on gasoline, new automobiles, tires, mechanical refrigerators, playing cards, club dues, toilet preparations and some others I have forgotten.

Poppa says that is not much compared to England. Their entire income is taxed at $42\frac{1}{2}$%. And it is just deducted from their wages!

So, Momma says, if a family made $70.00 a week, the pay check would only be $40.25.

Next week, you'll see me instead of a letter!
Much love from your friend
Eliza

Chapter XXXIX

SALLY COMES HOME!

Sally shows me the splint on her right side. It goes from her hip and includes her foot and it makes her foot stick straight up. The splint is open though and she can get in the bath tub and bounce around on her left foot, if she's careful. She goes for massages twice a week.

"Sally, do you remember how you got sick?" I want her to tell me what happened to her. I just want her to talk to me.

"You remember the day before your birthday when we went riding and then to the picture show? And you spent the night? Well, when I woke up that morning, my legs were sort of numb, but the numbness went away in the day. I thought maybe they were numb because I had slept in some new underpants and the elastic was too tight. Then, later that day, after you went home, I got a horrible headache and my legs were aching. I thought maybe we had ridden too long. Then, the next morning, Thursday, I had a high fever when I woke up and Mamma called the doctor. He came and said it was probably malaria and gave me some quinine which tastes terrible. Next day, Friday, I was worse and couldn't even put my leg over the tub to take a bath. So Mamma called the doctor back and said she feared I might have infantile paralysis. He said he had not seen many cases and so he called an ambulance to take us to the hospital. The ambulance driver was scared of polio, so our rector from church drove us. The specialist, Dr. Lupin, met us at the hospital, and he had me put my hands behind my back and he put a quarter in one hand and I couldn't tell which hand it was in. Then, he said I had infantile paralysis. Dr. Lubin then did a puncture on my spine and the pressure and pain were gone and I thought I was well!" Sally takes a sip of lemonade.

"But that was only the beginning. I was taken to the isolation hospital. And they moved an iron lung into my room! I cried and cried. I could feel my legs losing feeling, starting with my feet. I could not move. It was a horror! One night there was a mouse on my bedside table! Mamma and Daddy had a private nurse for me, but the doctors were short of help so she was often out of my room and she was gone when the mouse came."

"Oh, no! I would have been afraid to go to sleep," I shiver with the shivers that only a mouse can bring.

"I don't remember how much I slept. I did hear the Forest Hill Milk delivery truck every morning, with the horses' clumping feet coming down the street. I had therapy every day, and of course, Mamma came every day and sat outside my window. One day, Daddy brought a ladder so she could see me better and I could see her and she stayed there almost all day. It was a terrible hot day and she had a heat stroke!"

"Oh, no! Did she fall off the ladder?"

"I don't know; I don't think so. I'm just so glad to be home! I almost forgot how my room looked. And I really like my personally autographed Deanna Durbin picture. Get it out of my suitcase and pin it up for me, right there," Sally points, "so I can see it. I also liked your letters. In fact, I got lots of letters and cards. Everybody was so nice to me. Daddy says I can get all the way well if I will try."

"As if you wouldn't," I say with all truth.

The doorbell rings and Sally's mother's voice floats upstairs, "Why, hello, girls! Come in! I know Sally will be happy to see you."

Margaret, Catherine, Suzanna, Mimsy, Della and Renee squeeze into the room. "I brought you some crayons and a coloring book, because I always like to color when I am sick ... no matter how old I am!" explains Suzanna.

"Mimsy and I brought you some body lotion. It's 'Heaven Scent'," offers Della.

"All the boys like it," Mimsy adds. "You can use it when we start ballroom dancing class."

The whole room goes quiet.

"I don't know about ballroom dancing class," I look directly at Sally. "I would have written you if I did."

"Oh, everybody in Miss Meriwether's sixth grade always starts Miss Adelaide Nagel's classes on Friday night," Margaret says with authority. Then, she stops to look at Sally. "Oh, I forgot, I don't know whether you can dance or not."

"I don't either," says Sally looking at Margaret straight in the eye. "But if I can't right now, I bet I will be able to before too long. Daddy says I can get well if I try. And I've got all of you all to help me try. Tell more about Miss Adelaide's.

"I think, first, we have to get Sally back at school," says Catherine, "and this year you two are not the 'new girls'. What did the doctor say about your getting to school?"

"He'll tell me next week," says Sally.

"Even if you can't start right away, I'll bring you your lessons every day," I say with a claim on Sally.

"We all can help her with her homework. We can each take a different day," says Margaret, "I'll take Friday."

"You are all such good friends. I can't thank you enough for everything," and Sally wearily waves us goodbye.

I try to hang around and be the last one to say goodbye, but Margaret says, "It's time to let Sally rest, Eliza. Come on."

—〰—

"Well," says Poppa looking over his paper and his glasses, "I know you are happy to have your friend home."

"Yes, Poppa. She did tell me about getting sick and then half the class came to see her."

"That's good to hear. Sally will need all her friends to keep her morale up." Poppa puts his paper down. "You do know that, don't you? It's sort of like the English with the Home Guard. Over a million people have joined to help protect their country against invasion. The men in the Home Guard drill and practice; the women have gathered all their unusable pots and pans to be melted down; and they make tea and sing together as they endure the long night air-raids."

"What do they sing?" I ask Poppa.

"One song I remember:

> *Put up thumbs up and say it's Tiggerty Boo!*
> *We're going to show the world who's who.*
> *And this is how you end your little chorus:*
> *Thumb's up, Tiggerty Boo, Tiggerty Boo!*

It's the being in a tough spot ... not by yourself ... but having others there with you. That's what helps the most."

"I know, but I'm Sally's best friend and now Margaret is going to the ten cent store to buy her new notebook and stuff," I reveal. "And they didn't tell us about Miss Adelaide's Friday Night Ballroom Dancing Class. I'm not going to go if Sally can't go. Then, everybody will see who really is Sally's truest friend."

Chapter XL

THE SIXTH GRADE

"Welcome back, my dears and my darlings! And I am glad to announce that Sally will be returning to school as soon as the hottest weather is over. Is that right, Eliza? You two do come to school together?"

"Yes, Mrs. Freeland." I am satisfied at the public notice that I am the one who has the inside-Sally-story. "We usually walk, but our mothers will drive us for a while."

"Fine. Now let us have some summer reports. Yes, Renee?"

Renee rises, "Two things: one about the Dionne quintuplets. They are six years old and have just made their first communion. They were on the cover of *Life* a few weeks ago, in their white dresses and veils. They are Roman Catholic, you know. I am too."

"The second thing has to do with Paris," Renee continues, "the Swastika flies over Paris; but Paris was not destroyed. Rotterdam, Holland, was completely destroyed in two and one half hours, between noon and 2:30 pm on May 14th. Twenty-six thousand buildings in ruins; sewer pipes and canal machinery smashed. Thousands of people trapped in bomb shelters as buildings fell. Then, they either drowned from the smashed water mains and canals or they were roasted alive by the fires that had been set by incendiary bombs. That is so terrible and I am thankful that beautiful Paris had the sense to surrender and not be destroyed."

"Thank you, Renee. And is your uncle safe?"

"Yes, Mrs. Freeland. But I am not allowed to say where he is."

"Class, there is a final horror about the destruction of Rotterdam. The destruction was needless. The Dutch General, Winkelmann, had already surrendered! I read that the Germans told him that if planes came over, a red flare would signal the surrender to them. The planes came. Red flares went up. The planes bombed anyway and came back to bomb again! When Winkelmann made this fact known, he was arrested and has since disappeared into Germany." Mrs. Freeland pauses and looks at us as though trying to decide whether to continue. She sighs and adds, "The terrible lesson of Rotterdam had the effect the Germans wanted. Since then, no continental city has resisted the Germans."

"But, the English are resisting!" I rise to speak. "Two thousand five hundred Nazi planes bombed Britain one night, and Britain bombed back! One hundred Nazi cities and even the heart of Berlin. The port of Hamburg is practically in ruins. Of course, the RAF tried to hit only military targets. Whereas, the Nazi's hit a wing of Buckingham Palace! And the King and Queen still made their regular rounds the next morning among the burned buildings and rubble of London. The children are all gone though."

"We may have some refugee children here in Memphis," says Della. "Memphis has applied for 50 of the children, from all walks of life, and we have also offered to take their dogs."

"I read about what's happening to the dogs in Germany," adds Mimsy. "By order of the government, dog owners have been systematically killing their pets over the last three months. The only ones permitted to live are the work dogs used by the army, police, or Red Cross ... mostly dobermans and German shepherds. No dachshunds or schnauzers left."

"Why? Why?" there is a chorus.

"Mimsy, can you tell us why?" asks Mrs. Freeland.

"I guess because food is scarce and rationed and the dogs would starve or be eaten," answers Mimsy, "Knowing the 'why' does make the story more accurate, Mrs. Freeland, otherwise it just sounds like the government ordered the dogs to be killed for no reason."

"Well thought out, Mimsy. Eliza, in answer to your report about the British bombing only military targets in Germany, that may be the aim, but it is a very difficult thing to do. There are always civilian casualties and destruction of homes and churches," Mrs. Freeland adds.

"The *Life* cover girl on September 16, was a girl from Memphis, Jessie Woods. She was helping install the propeller on a plane that was making a flight across America," reports Mimsy, "also, about Memphis, the official count of the Census has come in and we have grown! We have almost 40,000 more people than ten years ago. My daddy says that is good news and he hopes at least ten per cent of them will want to buy a car from him."

"You have done well, class! That wasn't too hard, was it, to have a little work to do in August?" asks Mrs. Freeland.

"We did have some books to read for English. You know, 'the summer reading list,' says Mary Louise quietly.

"And we were also encouraged to memorize some poetry because Mrs. Hughes says we are the right age to memorize lovely things because our memorizers are at their peak and we will never forget what we memorize now."

"So, do I hear you saying that each teacher thinks hers is the only subject?" Mrs. Freeland laughs.

We sort of laugh back and say, "Yes."

"It has always been that way and I don't think it is likely to change! I guess you all could call that a 'universal.'"

Chapter XLI

FRIDAY NIGHT BALLROOM DANCING CLASS

"Your new dress is super. I like the full skirt."

"I like yours, too."

"You've rolled your hair differently."

"You have new shoes."

"Yes, but I think socks look babyish with them."

"I'm asking for stockings for Christmas and a garter belt!"

Everyone hears Della say this and the chatter ceases.

"What a super idea! Why don't we all do that? You know how Mothers check with each other. I'll surely ask my mother. Anyway, I think if we can wear Tangee Natural lipstick, we can certainly wear stockings." Suzanna has a proper sense of fashion which we all respect.

Miss Adelaide enters the room. We get quiet, even the boys on the other side of the room. I have tried not to look at them because I don't want them to think I am too interested. Bill says not to let a boy know too much.

"Next time, when you first come in the door, you will look for me," instructs Miss Adelaide, "You will look right straight into my eyes and say, 'Good evening, Miss Adelaide. I am so-and-so,' and then each young lady will make a slight curtsey and each young gentleman will extend his right hand. We shall now practice that. We shall begin over here, first a young lady and then a young gentleman.

Please speak up and say your name as though you are proud of it. Remember now, look at me straight in the eye. That's nice. Very good," as we alternate a boy and then a girl."

I don't know all the boys, but some are in my Sunday School class, two are from Davis, Tommy and Hugh. I can't wait to tell Sally. I'm sure that will make her come next time. Drew isn't here though. Della says since he is a year older, he is in the Saturday night class. Seventh graders go on Saturday night.

"Now we shall do our first step. It is easy and fun. Watch my feet," Miss Adelaide says as she puts the needle on the record. "Now, we shall all practice. Everyone on the floor. You can look in the mirrors and see how you are going, but do not, I repeat, DO NOT, look at your feet. That's it! Very good! Isn't it a lovely step? No, DO NOT look at your feet. Look at yourself in the mirrors." The record ends and Miss Adelaide removes the arm. "Now, we will dance with partners."

Giggles from the girls and groans from the boys.

"This dance will be the step we just practiced and you young gentlemen will walk, not run, across the room and select a young lady to dance with and you will say, "So-and-so, may I have this dance?" More groans from the boys.

"And young ladies, you will take the offered hand and rise from your seat and say, 'Thank you, I would love to dance.' And then you will walk onto the floor, take your proper dancing positions and wait for the music."

Oh, I hope someone will ask me. I hadn't thought about the chance there might be more girls than boys. Suddenly Tommy and Hugh are right in front of me asking me to dance! I am so glad to see them, but I don't know what to do. Miss Adelaide appears like magic, "Eliza can only dance with one at a time. Hugh, you were there, first. Tommy, you may have the next dance. Eliza, you say 'thank you' and nod graciously to first one and then the other."

"There are more boys than girls tonight. Sometimes it is the other way around. But that does not matter. The idea is to enjoy dancing. If we have a young gentleman left over, he is allowed to dance with the broomstick so that he does not miss the practice of getting his feet used to the dance floor. As you become more at home with the music, you will enjoy making conversation. Animated conversation. Look as though you are having a good time, even though you are not yet quite sure. Yes, Roger, you can talk to the broomstick! Some young ladies don't have any more to say than a broomstick and you have to carry the whole thing!"

"Hey, Hugh, how is everybody at Davis?"

"Fine. You know the sixth grader is the big dog."

"Yes, I know. Who is your teacher?"

"Mrs. Wells. You remember? She's the one that whips boys in front of the class. She whipped Jerry Baum the other day because he wouldn't stand up straight and we all know he can't stand up straight."

"Oh, how awful! I would have cried. We have a teacher who calls us 'her dears and her darlings,' but she makes us work hard. It's not bad though."

"How is Sally?"

"Sally is doing so much better. I bet she's here next time. I'll tell her you asked."

The music stops. "Now, return your young lady to her seat and thank her for the dance and young ladies, you express your appreciation and look into the person's face when you speak. Very nice."

We learn some more steps and different boys dance with the broom and the girls always have a partner. This is fun!

"See you next week," Tommy says as he returns me to my seat after the last dance.

Chapter XLII

THE DRUG STORE

"Well, Margaret and Renee tell me you were the most popular one! That the boys raced, not walked, across the room to ask you to dance," Sally's eyes are sparkling wide.

"I don't see it that way, but I did have a really good time! I wore the red and black plaid taffeta dress that my cousin, Betty, had outgrown and sent to me. I love the way it goes in at the waist."

"Was anybody a wallflower?" whispers Sally.

"No. We had more boys than girls so every girl danced everytime. It would be so embarrassing to be left sitting on the bench." I shudder. "But, Sally, you have got to come. Hugh asked how you were and I told him you would probably be there next time. What did the doctor say yesterday?"

"I can go to school this week for a half-day!"

"That's super. Will you use crutches?"

"Yes."

"I'll carry your books. No, I guess I'll offer to carry your books but probably everybody will want to help."

The telephone rings. "Sally, it's for you," calls Mrs. Long.

Sally hops on her left leg to the phone, "Oh, hey, Hugh."

Gosh, am I glad I'm here!

"I'm doing great. I'm going to school half-day this week. What? Oh, that's nice of you. I'll have to ask Mama." Sally rolls her eyes at me.

"Mama," she calls," Hugh wants to know if I can go to the drug store with him after dancing class next Friday?"

Mrs. Long appears at the door. "Is that the drug store right down the street from Miss Adelaide's?" Mrs. Long lowers her voice to a whisper, "Do you want to go?"

Sally nods yes.

"Well, your daddy and I can pick you up from the drug store then."

"I can go, Hugh. Thank you. Oh, really? That's good," Sally is looking at me and grinning. "No, I won't tell her," and she shows me her crossed fingers. "Well, bye."

"Eliza, Tommy's going to call you to go too!"

"Sally, is this a date? Mamma says you have to be fourteen at least."

"No, I don't think it's a date; it's just the drug store. I won't be able to dance I don't think. But it's just fun to be there with everybody and I can learn some of the steps by watching."

"What will we get at the drug store?" I ask.

"I guess ice cream or a coke," answers Sally.

"I love sodas," I confess.

When I get home, Momma tells me Tommy has called. "Am I to call him back?" I ask.

"No, Eliza. Girls don't as a rule call boys. Unless, you are calling for a specific reason, for example, to ask him to escort you to a party. Tommy said he would call back. He seems like a nice boy." Momma looks at me. "Did you enjoy dancing school?"

"Momma, it was wonderful! You know I love to dance and I guess all that ballet and tap have paid off because ballroom does not seem hard. Lots of boys asked me."

"It is always fun to be sought after. But every girl has a time when no one asks her to dance," Momma says.

"And she is left sitting on the bench?"

"Yes, for some reason, it happens to everybody. I guess that is good because then we don't get to thinking we are too cute and everything is always going our way." Momma is using psychology on me again.

"Hugh asked Sally to go the drug store after dancing class. He told her that Tommy was going to ask me. Mrs. Long said Sally can go. Can I go?"

"Do you want to go?"

"Yes, Momma. But what do I get at the drug store?"

"You don't get anything that costs more than a nickel. Because, you see, you don't know how much Tommy has to spend."

"Momma, I love sodas and they cost ten cents. What if he asks me if I would like a soda? Am I supposed to say 'no'?"

"Yes. I think it would be best to say that you would like an ice cream cone and then choose your favorite flavor. Truly, men appreciate it when women are thoughtful of their pocketbooks," Momma says with her wisdom look. "Remember, he wants to have enough left to buy something for himself. Oh, good news. Gamma is coming home tomorrow!"

"But I really do like sodas. You really mean I have to say 'no' even if he asks, 'Eliza, are you sure you don't want a soda? I know you like them. I am going to have a soda.' Even then?"

Momma looks a little uncertain.

I feel a dent in the parental fortress. I press my case. "I thought you and Poppa told me always to tell things exactly the way they are, then I would not have to remember what I said."

"I suppose there are exceptions to every rule," admits Momma.

"But in general, a girl is wise to choose the least expensive item on the menu or next to least, but never the most. Do you want to go with us to meet Gamma at the train station?"

Chapter XLIII

SHALL WE ELECT A PRESIDENT TO A THIRD TERM?

"Sally, we've been eager for you to come back and to hear your report on the upcoming election for president of the United States," Mrs. Freeland leads the class in a welcoming round of applause. "You may sit, if it is easier for you, but that means you have to project your voice even more and be sure to look around at the class and make eye contact with your listeners."

"Yes, Mrs. Freeland. Well, as you know, the two main candidates are Mr. Wendell Willkie and Mr. Franklin Delano Roosevelt who is running for a third term! The first time any president has ever done that! He is the candidate for the Democratic ticket. His vice presidential running mate is Mr. Henry Wallace."

"Shall someone write those names on the board for you?" asks Mrs. Freeland.

"Yes. That is a good idea. Eliza, you got my assignment for me, so will you?"

I love to write on the blackboard.

"I'm having a hard time understanding whether Mr. Wallace is a member of the Democratic Party or the Republican Party. He was Secretary of Agriculture under President Herbert Hoover, who was a Republican, and then he was also Secretary of Agriculture under Mr. Roosevelt, who, as I just said, is a Democrat. Anyhow,

Mr. Roosevelt wanted Mr. Wallace for his vice-president, but the rest of the Democratic Party did not like his choice."

"Do you know how they were nominated, Sally?"

"A little bit, but it does seem complicated, Mrs. Freeland. The Democratic Party had a nominating convention in Chicago on July 15, right after I got sick. Mr. Roosevelt had never actually said he wanted a third term, but my daddy said he refused to support another candidate. And that he did not discourage efforts on his behalf."

I am waiting to write something else on the blackboard.

"The day after the convention opened, July 16, the president sent them a message that he had no desire to remain in office. He said he wanted the convention to be free to choose, but he hinted he would accept the nomination if chosen. My daddy said he was talking out of both sides of his mouth."

"So what happened?" asks Margaret who is always interested in elections.

"The convention had no choice, the paper said, but to nominate him on the first ballot," concludes Sally.

"Why did they not have a choice? Could they not have nominated someone else and told Mr. Roosevelt he had said to do that?" asks Margaret.

"No, not really. Because the president in office is the head of the party," explains Mrs. Freeland.

"So, he didn't mean what he said?" asks Margaret again.

"My poppa doesn't like Mr. Roosevelt," I blurt out. "Although he respects the office of president," I add quickly.

"Maybe he didn't want the country getting into a big discussion about his third term," Mary Louise suggests.

"Anyway, everyone now says that the world is in a dangerous situation and we must not change horses in mid-stream," adds Mimsy.

"Well, Mimsy, that is funny, because Mr. Wendell Willkie, who is the Republican candidate for President says:

The closer Mr. Roosevelt gets us to war, the more people say we ought not to change horses in the middle of the stream. How did we get there? The man who got us in it is not the right one to get us out!

Who knows who is right? I sure don't," and Sally concludes her report for that day.

"Very nice, Sally. Next week, you might like to tell us about the Republican nominating convention and how Mr. Willkie was nominated. And class, we have this new term to watch for: 'selective service.' Class dismissed."

"Sally, are you going to the horse show? We have tickets for opening night! Everybody is going to be there. Is your daddy showing his Tennessee Walking Horse?" Margaret asks as she picks up Sally's books and walks in front of me.

Chapter LXIV

'WAIT AND SEE'

"We have a holiday today!"

"It's nice to have a holiday when the weather is lovely and the sky so blue. October weather is the best," declares Gamma.

"Well, I don't like it because it means the days are getting shorter and then winter is coming and it will be dark before five o'clock," Poppa responds. "Why have you a holiday, Eliza? On October 16th? Oh, I forgot. Registration for selective service. At each neighborhood school. I did see where the teachers and principals were volunteering their time and clerical skills to be in charge of the registration. And Miss Meriwether's is closed too?"

"Yes, Poppa. There's a meeting to work out the placing of the 50 refugee children that are coming to Memphis. Mrs. Freeland's on the committee. You and Bill don't have to register, do you, Poppa?"

"No. The ages are 21 to 36."

"Gamma, tell us about Uncle Henry and everything."

"Your Uncle Henry is very happy. He and Amy make a distinguished couple."

"And Aunt Lucy?"

"Aunt Lucy is fine and busy as usual. She has applied to take a brother and sister refugee pair, hopefully with a dog. Probably will know this week. She sent you lots of hugs and love and 'sympathy.'"

I laugh. "Did you see Frances or any of my camper friends?"

"Yes, the carpool stopped by one day to say 'hello' and to send you greetings. And to hear about your train adventure and your quarantine."

"Did you get to Providence and see where the eighth step had been tampered with?"

"I did. And it had been repaired. Your Uncle Henry is very thorough, as you know, and he had had the damaged step itself and the inside part of it photographed by a photographer and he had all of it dusted for finger prints."

"Why didn't he write us that?"

"I guess because there was not any treasure."

"Were there finger prints?" I ask.

"Yes, the finger prints belonged to Gus."

"Oh, I thought Gus was suspicious," I confess.

"It is strange how we think anyone who is different is suspicious," observes Gamma. "His prints were there because he was the one who had repaired and painted the steps earlier."

"So, is there still a mystery? What about the rings?"

"Well, Aunt Lucy has one and Lucy has the other and that is all there is to it. Uncle Henry says we should forget it. In just those words."

"I bet Uncle Henry is protecting Gus." I notice Bill has been listening throughout. "Don't you think so, Bill?"

"I don't think Uncle Henry would stand for dishonesty for one moment. So, Gus must be in the clear. Uncle Henry may know something we don't though. You know how quiet he is. He hates gossip and chatter. Who knows?" Bill observes.

"Well, I hope Aunt Lucy gets her refugee children and dog. Won't they have fun at the apple orchard?"

"In the summer, surely. But the winters are snow bound and Aunt

Lucy doesn't have other children close by for them to play with. Little Compton even practices black outs now," reveals Gamma. "We'll just have to wait and see."

"Why do grown-ups always say that?" I ask Gamma impatiently.

"Because that is the way it is, Eliza. For example, each man who registers today will be given a number. The numbers will all be put in a 'pot' and then drawn out one at a time and the men will be called up in that order. So, those who registered will just have to wait and see."

"I wouldn't. If I were old enough to have to register, I wouldn't wait for the lottery. I'd volunteer. And then have some choice in my branch of the service," says Bill, "I wouldn't wait and see."

"What makes everyone do as he is told? Suppose someone doesn't want to register?" I ask.

"Oh, that's easy. A fine of $10,000.00 or five years imprisonment or both, if you don't," explains Bill.

"Well, what service would you volunteer for?" I hadn't realized that Bill had thought about it.

"Probably the paratroopers or the Air Force," Bill answers.

"You have the courage to jump out of a plane?"

"You are trained, you know. In how to jump and how to fall, all the essentials," Bill replies.

"I still would be afraid to jump. I'm not even brave in the dentist's chair. I read that Hitler seldom shows his teeth because they are bad. That he seldom visits a dentist because he is afraid of being hurt. Do you suppose that is true?" I ask.

"I have no idea. And I don't give a hoot about Hitler's teeth," laughs Bill.

Chapter XLV

THE PRESIDENTIAL ELECTION

"I think we are too young to have a date after dancing school, don't you?" Margaret is the center of the group as Sally and I approach. "I think that should be something we do in the seventh grade. I think anybody that does that now is ... 'fast.' Oh, hello, Sally and Eliza. We are all agreeing that we shouldn't go to the drug store with a boy after dancing school until the seventh grade."

"Our mothers said it was all right," I answer. "Did your mother make you tell someone you couldn't go?"

"Well, no. No one actually asked me, but I know I wouldn't be allowed to. We are all agreeing that it isn't in good taste to do that in the sixth grade," Margaret continues.

"Della, Mimsy, Suzanna, is that what your mothers said?" asks Sally.

"Mother hasn't said anything because nobody has asked me. I guess Tommy and Hugh asked you all because you all were in the same class at Davis and they were glad to see you again," observes Della.

"Or maybe public schools kids are faster," chimes in Margaret.

"Good morning, class," Mrs. Freeland's presence ends the drug store conversation.

"Sally, tell us about Mr. Wendell Willkie, the Republican candidate for president."

"The Republican Convention was in Philadelphia in May. May 24, to be exact, two days after the surrender of France. Daddy thinks that is the reason Senator Robert Taft of Ohio was not nominated. Senator Taft is a non-interventionist, but there was panic in the air after France's surrender. Mr. Willkie's managers were able to get support for him because he has a more internationalist viewpoint. It took four days of balloting. And Mrs. Freeland, Mr. Willkie used to be a Democrat!"

"That is interesting, isn't it class?"

"Like horses changing streams," quips Mary Louise.

"The election next week promises to be very close. Mr. Willkie actually agrees with most of Mr. Roosevelt's policies, domestic as well as foreign. He even supported the president in getting the draft bill signed in September. Then some of his Old Guard professional politicians begged Willkie to stop talking about a 'bi-partisan' foreign policy and attack Roosevelt as a 'War-monger' and scare the American people that votes for Roosevelt would mean war," explains Mrs. Freeland.

"What is bi-partisan, Mrs. Freeland?"

"It means cooperation or agreement between two major political parties," Mrs. Freeland replies.

"Please give us an example," requests Mimsy.

"Bi-partisan means the Republicans and the Democrats working together to get a bill passed. Often during a war, the two major parties will put aside the things on which they disagree and work together to win the war."

"And then as soon as peace is signed, they start fighting again?"

"And it doesn't seem to me that either party plays exactly fair," comments Mary Louise.

"Actually, the president spoke in Boston last night and the speech was broadcast on the radio:

'I have said this before, but I will say it again and again: Your boys are not going to be sent into any foreign wars ... The purpose of our defense is defense.'"

"But does he mean it, Mrs. Freeland?" I ask. "Does he mean that we will not fight in a war?"

"I think Mr. Roosevelt means that the defense of Britain is the same as the defense of the United States. That helping Britain is not a foreign war."

"How many people will vote?" asks Renee. "I know Margaret told me there are 50 million registered to vote."

"Poppa says there is a lot of 'political pep' right now. Wouldn't everybody vote unless they were sick?" I ask.

"I've seen pictures of some signs against a third term," offers Mimsy:

**In Russia
It's the THIRD INTERNATIONAL**

**In Germany
It's the THIRD REICH**

**In America
There must be
NO THIRD TERM**

---

and also:

**HITLER WAS ELECTED
THE FIRST 3 TIMES
VOTE NO ON THIRD TERM
DICTATORSHIP**

"Thank you, Mimsy. Does anyone know what an electoral vote is?"

"Yes, I mean, I think so. For example, Tennessee has 11 electoral votes; Rhode Island has four and New York has 47," I offer what Bill had explained to me the night before. "Obviously, it is more important to win in New York than in Tennessee or Rhode Island."

"Right, Eliza. But what does the electoral vote represent?"

"I know," says Suzanna, "the number represents the number of members of the House of Representatives, which is based on that state's population, plus the two senators. Tennessee has nine representatives and has two senators, so we have eleven electoral votes."

"What if Tennessee casts 112,000 votes for Willkie and 113,000 for Mr. Roosevelt, the winner would still get all eleven electoral votes?" is a question from the floor.

"That is right. Think a minute. Can you see how it would be possible for the man elected president, the man who got the most electoral votes, could actually have received fewer popular votes than the loser?" queries Mrs. Freeland. "Think about it. And next time see if you can tell me how many electoral votes a candidate needs to be elected."

"Tennessee is a Democratic state; it will vote Democratic. Wasn't Abraham Lincoln a Republican?" Margaret looks around to see if everyone has heard her.

Chapter XLVI

A DIFFERENT KIND OF NEW GIRL

"Eliza, can you spend the night Friday and stay most of the day Saturday?" Catherine's eyes are dancing. "You can call me tonight after you ask your mother."

"I'm sure I can, Catherine. Are you 'dining-in'?"

"Yes. This is something very special. Mother and Father both said they would like for you to come. You don't suppose Bill would come to dinner? It's really special."

"I'll ask him. And he'll call you. What time?"

"At half-after-seven. But he might want to come about thirty minutes early."

"What do you suppose is so special?" wonders Bill half-aloud. "The elections aren't until Tuesday. Do you suppose Mr. Hunt is going to quiz us on the election or the situation in the Far East? I wish I knew what to bone-up on," as he heads to the phone. "What's Catherine's number?" He dials.

"Hello, Catherine. This is Bill, Eliza's brother. I'm fine, thank you. How about you? That's good. Well, my sister was telling me about your kind invitation to dinner. Something about something special? Well, thank you, I would be glad to come ... that is, if it is not storming!"

Momma pulls the Studebaker over the brick drive to the back-front door. Catherine runs out to greet us. "Mrs. Horton, meet our new English girl! This is Audrey Berrington-Jones. And Audrey, this is Eliza. She was a 'new girl' last year, but she is my friend now."

Audrey looks at Momma in the eye and shakes her hand. "How do you do, Mrs. Horton." And then, she turns to me, "How do you do, Eliza," looks me in the eye and shakes my hand.

"Catherine was the first person to speak to me when I was a 'new girl' and I shall never forget her," I say.

"We are glad to have you in our country, Audrey, and hope your stay will be one of as much contentment as possible, under the circumstances," and Momma gives her a straightforward mature look. "Bill is riding his bike over shortly, Catherine." And Momma waves goodbye.

"When did you arrive, Audrey?" I can hardly believe Catherine has an English refugee.

"They arrived here last night, but there were many stops before that and ... oh, here comes Bill!" exclaims Catherine. "Then Derrick and Audrey can tell us all at once."

"Your brother? And did you bring your dog?" I asked, thinking this would be the perfect family for Aunt Lucy.

"Yes, as a matter of fact, we were allowed to bring Winston," and as if on command, a large golden dog bounds from the house.

"Winston? That's Mr. Churchill's name."

"I know, we've had a razzing about that."

"Which room is yours?" I ask. This whole situation is extraordinary. Catherine did not tell me their family had applied for refugees.

"I am to take Daphne's room while she is away at school and when she comes home for holiday, I am to share with Catherine."

"And I have Robert's quarters with him or without him," laughs Derrick.

The dining room shines with the brilliance I remember. And Derrick and Bill seat the three girls. Mr. and Mrs. Hunt are beaming and so are James and Zora. Mrs. Muzzy-dear is on a one-week rest.

"And we thank God for the safe arrival of Audrey and Derrick," Mr. Hunt concludes the blessing.

"And we will do whatever we can to make you feel at home," adds Mrs. Hunt, "no, even more, to help you feel that we are a second family to you."

"Thank you, Mrs. Hunt," say both Audrey and Derrick almost together.

"Tell us about your coming," asks Catherine, "that is, if you want to."

"Yes, of course," responds Derrick. "You know when war first started, in September of last year, British children were taken from big cities to the countryside. We live in London, so we were sent to our Aunt Christina who lives in the country near Coventry. Then after the fall of France in May, there was fear of invasion, so it was decided to send the children ...."

"Those age five to fifteen," adds Audrey.

"That's right, Audrey. And I was just about to turn 15 ... to Canada and to the United States. Over 200,000 children applied. Much had to be done: families had to be found to care for the children ... and ships to transport them. One unescorted ship was torpedoed with loss of all the children."

"Oh, no!" I gasp.

"Yes. It was then decided it would be safer to send the children by convoy. But all the ships were needed for anti-invasion work, so the program was stopped. Actually on July 10."

"That's my birthday," the words just slip out.

"Oh. Well, the program was officially stopped but parents who could afford to send their children privately and were willing to take the risk, were allowed to do so."

"That was a big risk," Bill says.

"Everything in life is a risk," observes Mr. Hunt.

"There is a committee in the United States. I think your president's wife, Mrs. Roosevelt, is on that committee," says Audrey.

"My mother is too," adds Catherine. "That helped us be able to get you to come be our new family."

"Anyhow, to shorten the story, we wore our name tags, brought our birth certificates, ten pictures of ourselves, our gas masks, and two suitcases. I don't know how we were lucky enough to bring Winston." And Derrick starts to eat his soup.

I know it is not polite to mention money, but I wonder how much it cost Audrey's and Derrick's parents to send them and Winston. I wonder if they live in a mansion like the Hunt's or in a smaller, plainer one. I guess we can talk about that when we are not "dining-in."

"My Aunt Lucy, who lives in Rhode Island, asked for a boy and girl and a dog," I say. "But we haven't heard whether she got her wish."

"I doubt if she will, Eliza. The committee looks for a home that has a mother and a father and even tries to place, say a minister's children, in another minister's household," Bill says.

"Why didn't you tell me that before? Is that true, Mr. Hunt? But, what if the children had come from a house with only a mother?" I cannot believe that Aunt Lucy will be deprived of all of her wishes.

"You speak with fervor, Eliza. You must love this Aunt Lucy," Mr. Hunt looks at me intently. "Tell us about her."

"Well, Mr. Hunt, she is Bill's Aunt Lucy too and he loves her as much as I do."

Bill nods in agreement.

"She is so much fun. She runs an apple orchard in the country in Rhode Island, and she has two golden retrievers, and a shiny black Buick and a chauffeur named James." I glance a smile at James who is passing the vegetables. "She loves to play with us: checkers or double solitaire or to read to us. She writes stories too." I realize I have talked too long.

"Perhaps you will get to visit her again this next summer." Mr. Hunt turns to Catherine. "I understand your summer assignment from Mrs. Freeland was China. I remember your telling me that the United States had asked 16,000 U.S. citizens to leave the Orient. Do you know anything more recent?"

"Yes, Father. Just today. The first of American refugees sailed from Shanghai for home. Only two hundred, mostly women and children. The article said that the threat of war this time was not that of the Japanese/Chinese conflict to which we have gotten used to over the last three years, but a threat of war between Japan and the United States."

We have war on both sides of us! And refugees coming from both sides! But we still have the Atlantic and Pacific Oceans to guard us.

"Audrey, you will start school with Catherine and Eliza at Miss Meriwether's this Monday," explains Mrs, Hunt. "And Derrick, we still have to make the decision about your school. You would normally, of course, be with Robert, but he is away at school. You may do that, if you choose, but we were not content with the idea of separating you and your sister at this time in your lives."

"Bill, you attend a public school here, and I have been impressed with your demeanor and with your knowledge of the world around you. Do you think Derrick would find your school a challenging, but also a welcoming place?" queries Mr. Hunt.

"Yes, sir. I think so. I would be glad to be his sponsor if that is his decision."

Bill is so mature I can't stand it! Catherine is beaming at him.

"That's enough serious talk for one night. Shall we go see Judy Garland and Mickey Rooney in *Strike up the Band*?" And Mr. Hunt pushes back from the table.

"Lux Radio Theatre is going to have Judy and Mickey in Strike up the Band this Monday night on the radio," I say to Audrey.

"That's 'wireless' to you," Catherine explains to Audrey with a laugh.

Chapter XLVII

SOME WIN; SOME LOSE

"Today is election day, class. How many electoral votes does a candidate need to win?"

The class choruses "266!" Sally has coached us.

"Right! And we should know the results by tomorrow morning. I brought you a sample ballot cut out of this morning's paper. Notice how the 11 electors are listed under each candidate's name?"

"But who is Roger W. Babson, a candidate for President? And who is Mr. Thomas, a candidate for President? We haven't even mentioned them. They each have 11 electors also. What's going on?" asks Sally who is taking her assignment of reporting on the election very seriously.

Wednesday Sally brings the morning paper to class. Large headlines blare

ROOSEVELT AHEAD IN 38 STATES

"So, we don't really know who won yet or do we, Mrs. Freeland?"

"It looks as though Mr. Roosevelt will be elected to a third term and it also looks as though both the House of Representatives and the Senate will have Democratic majorities. Probably the afternoon paper will have the official statement. Can you think of different things that this election teaches us?"

"We have a president elected for a third term! That's terrible!"

says Margaret.

"If the election is close in popular votes, a lot of people are going to be disappointed or maybe even mad," observes Suzanna. "Does that mean our country will be divided?"

"It means," answers Mrs. Freeland, "that one of the problems facing America now is to erase any bitterness caused by the campaign. I do mean erase." Mrs. Freeland picks up the eraser and cleans the blackboard of all the candidates' names and other notes we had made. "Tomorrow we will write the new president's name on the board and support him because he is our elected leader."

"26,300,000 popular votes for Roosevelt. 22,000,000 popular votes for Willkie. 449 electoral votes for Roosevelt and 82 electoral votes for Willkie. I see what you mean, Mrs. Freeland. The popular vote is pretty close, but the electoral vote is not. I guess the states with the most electoral votes went for Roosevelt." Sally sounds like a news commentator. "I made a map that shows how the states voted and what each electoral count was. And Mrs. Freeland, did you see what Mr. McNary, Willkie's vice-presidential candidate, said?
I am wishing Mr. Roosevelt and Mr. Wallace, grace and their administration, prosperity. We shall try to furnish them a worthy and vigilant opposition.
Is that what you meant, Mrs. Freeland? The losers are good sports?"

"Yes, Sally, good sports for their own mental health because it hurts the one was carries the burden of a grudge, but more than good sports, 'A worthy and vigilant opposition'. That is, speaking up, constructively, when there are differences of opinion."

"Well, it's good to have the election behind us. We have other things to think about. Like Thanksgiving is coming and then Christmas and we start practicing for the Christmas Choral Group Concert this weekend. Audrey, would you like to come with Sally and me? We are in the Children's Choir at our church," I say.

"Thank you, Eliza. Where do you go to church?"

"It's downtown. It is an Episcopal church."

"I could go then, if it is all right with Mrs. Hunt. The Episcopal Church is just about the same as the Church of England, which I attend at home. Except you pray for the president and we pray for the King."

"We could pray for both," I say. "Good. Choir practice is tomorrow after school. You'll love it! Momma will drive us."

We gather around Mr. Huffman's big grand piano and start with "Silent Night." I love Christmas carols and I know all the verses to every single one. I sing and sing. So does Audrey. She has a lovely voice. A good addition to our choir. Next: 'O Little Town of Bethlehem, how still we see thee lie, above thy deep and dreamless sleep the silent stars go by..' Oh, I love it!
I love it!

Suddenly, Mr. Huffman stops playing, pushes back the piano bench and rises to his feet. "Let us sing this a capella, children. You know, without any accompaniment. How about 'O Come All Ye Faithful'?" He strikes a note on the piano to give us a start. Then he walks around our circle with his ear close to first one and then another. I am singing my heart out. He gets to me and stops. I give him smiling eyes and sing even louder.

"You," he says. Everyone stops singing. He points a finger at me, "you have got to go!"

Chapter XLVIII

ELIZA LICKS HER WOUNDS

"Oh, Momma," I let the tears flow, "I was so humiliated. I have my perfect attendance pins. I know all the words. I have never even been tardy. And I love to sing in the choir! Oh, Momma! I thought I was going to die!" I sob. "I had even taken Audrey as a special guest and she is a new member and I am not a member anymore." I howl with pain. "I don't think I can go to Sunday School anymore. Everybody will see I'm not in the choir and will ask me why." I howl more.

"There, there," Momma pats me and hugs me. "What a hurtful thing to have happen. I can't imagine what Mr. Huffman was thinking of. You have been an enthusiastic and faithful member."

"I know, Momma," says Bill, "but she can't sing. She can't carry the tune to 'Row, row, row your boat.' But that was a cruel thing to do in front of all the choir. Why didn't he just ask her to mouth the words?"

"Awww!" I howl more, "That would ... hiccup ... be just as bad."

The phone rings. "It's for you, Eliza. It's Sally."

"What happened today at choir was so terrible. Audrey and I are not going anymore if you can't be in the choir," Sally's voice is stricken.

"Oh, you're not?" I begin to come to. "Then Mr. Huffman cannot have her lovely new English voice and your tried and true voice. He'll be sorry he was so mean to me."

"Maybe the whole choir will quit because he was so cruel," Sally is conjuring up sweet revenge.

"Wouldn't that be wonderful? It would teach him a thing or two," I can picture there being no procession of children behind the crucifer. All because he was so mean. "Well, Minerva says dinner is ready. So I've got to go. Bye."

"I hear you had a tough time today at choir practice," Poppa says as he carves the meat. "I trust you held your manners and composure until you reached the privacy of your home."

"Yes, Poppa, I did. I didn't say anything and I didn't cry. That is until I got home. But Sally is going to fix it so nobody goes to choir because he was so mean to me."

"Sally is your loyal friend."

"Yes, Poppa. We'll show him."

"I wonder what would happen if all the Republicans 'stayed at home' because the Democrats won the White House, and the House of Representatives and the Senate?" muses Poppa.

"Yes, Poppa. Mrs. Freeland talked about being good sports and erasing all bitterness and being, let me see if I can remember, she made us copy it down, oh, I know, 'a worthy and vigilant opposition.'"

"Mrs. Freeland is a wise teacher. I have heard it said: 'The longer we dwell on our misfortunes, the greater is their power to harm us'. Do you want gravy?"

"Yes, please. Well, it would be sad if every junior choir member had to stop singing because I couldn't carry a tune," I admit. "But he was so mean."

"Mr. Huffman was thoughtless and I am going to call him and have a chat with him," says Momma.

"You are not going to ask him to take me back, are you, Momma? I would die!"

"No. Choosing the choir members is his job not mine," replies Momma. "Now, let's talk about something else."

"Well, I know something exciting," says Gamma. "The city's first streamliner is coming to Central Station tomorrow. Shall we go see it? The mayor's daughter is going to christen it."

"With a bottle of champagne? Like the ships?" asks Bill.

"No.. with a pint of brown Mississippi River water. Right on the big red Diesel engine," triumphantly responds Gamma, who doesn't approve of alcoholic beverages.

Chapter XLIX

"A STIFF UPPER LIP"

"Hitler said it was 'a thousandfold' reprisal for the bombing of Munich. More than a million pounds of bombs smashed parts of Coventry, as flat as Rotterdam," says Renee.

Catherine and I turn to look at Audrey. She is sitting up straight in her desk, looking into space, not blinking an eye.

"Isn't Audrey's Aunt Christina near Coventry?" I whisper.

"Yes," answers Catherine.

"Yes, Audrey. You have your hand up?" Mrs. Freeland says.

Audrey rises to her feet and speaks in her beautiful English voice. "There was significant action in the Mediterranean Sea yesterday. British planes torpedoed half of Italy's warships in a daring harbor attack. The morning news said that the blow would alter the balance of power in the Mediterranean. This is not propaganda news for there is photographic evidence of the victory." Audrey sits down and she does not mention Coventry.

"Mrs. Freeland, the schools and a college in Shreveport, Louisiana, have been closed until after Thanksgiving because of six cases of infantile paralysis," Sally reports. "And it's not even hot weather!"

"I'm sorry to hear that, Sally, but we are all glad that you continue to improve. Speaking of Thanksgiving, class," Mrs. Freeland smiles,

"Tennessee is celebrating on the last Thursday again. And the Junior Red Cross is being re-activated. Margaret has been appointed to head up your chapter for the rest of the year, and her committee has met. Margaret, would you like to report?"

Margaret stands and looks so smirky I could spit. I think I'll write that in the Slam Book on her page. Maybe I'm not sorry I still have that red book hidden at home. I can write everything I feel about Margaret ... in different handwriting ... and then put the book in her desk!

"Our first project is a food basket for an unfortunate family. Audrey, I bet you don't have Thanksgiving Day in England so will you be on the committee so you can see what it is?"

"Thank you, Margaret. But you must tell me what to do," responds Audrey.

Don't I know Margaret would love to tell her what to do! Why didn't Margaret ask for volunteers? I would like to help get food for a poor family, but maybe they are going to serenade and I might throw them off key.

"I would like to help," says Catherine, "and if there is extra driving, I know Mother would allow James to take us."

"Maybe the whole class is interested, Margaret?" suggests Mrs. Freeland.

There is a chorus of agreement. "How do we find a family?" asks Mary Louise.

"The Red Cross gave us a name and address and the names and ages of the children. And a list of things that would be nice to put in the basket," explains Margaret.

"Could we raise our own money and not just ask our parents for it? Have the basket really be from us?" suggests Suzanna.

"There's not much time to earn money between now and

Thanksgiving, but I have saved up allowance because I was quarantined and couldn't go to the movie," I say.

"Could we each bring as much as a dollar?"

"We'll just see what we can do."

Fourteen class members pile their money on Mrs. Freeland's desk and are counting when she comes in with a grocery ad from the paper. We have $8.80!

"Audrey, you are good with math. Will you make the tally?"

Audrey writes as we tell her:

20 pound turkey @ 22¢/lb	$4.40
2 doz. large oranges @ 18¢/doz	.36
2 tins cranberry sauce @ 11½¢	.23
2 dozen eggs @ 25¢	.50
2 lbs. marshmallows @ 10¢	.20
24 lbs Blue Bunny Flour	.89
2 lbs brown sugar @ 6½¢	.13
6 lbs sweet potatoes @ 2½¢	.15
12 winesap apples @ 1¢ each	.12
4 cans whole green beans @ 13½¢	.54
5 lbs onions @ 2¢	.10
2 stalks of celery @ 5¢	.10
box of salt	.02
3 dozen dinner rolls at 5¢	.15
2 large cans of peaches @ 2/23¢	.23
1 lb of Maxwell House coffee	.23
1 jar peanut butter	.10
TOTAL	$8.58

"Hurray! we have enough and even 22¢ left over!"

"We could get an Angel Food cake for 15¢. And a pound of red grapes for 5¢ and we would be almost exactly even!" I know about important things like the cost of cakes.

"But what about milk? Children have to have milk."

"And a pumpkin? for pumpkin pie."

"The dairy delivers milk and cream. Could somebody leave a note for the milkman?"

"I would like to make that my contribution," claims Mrs. Freeland.

"Oh, thank you, Mrs. Freeland. I didn't know you were part of our Junior Red Cross," says Margaret.

"I guess you might call me the adult sponsor, but you all have done such a caring job that I want to be a part of your gift."

"That only leaves the pumpkin."

"Well, they will have angel cake for dessert."

"But the Pilgrims had pumpkin pie, not angel cake."

"They had corn too, and we are not buying any corn. We are not even getting corn meal for the turkey dressing."

"Maybe they have some corn meal."

We meet at Catherine's and James drives us in the Packard station wagon to the grocery store. It is the neatest car. It is part wood and part metal. The inside ceiling is wooden strips and the body is rubbed wood. The fenders and hood are dubonnet red and so are the leather seats. "This motor car doesn't have a boot," observes Audrey.

"A boot?" we all say.

"Audrey and Derrick call the 'trunk', the 'boot', and the 'hood', the 'bonnet'."

"That's funny. But we all speak English, right?"

"Right-o!" answers Audrey.

Back at Catherine's, we pack the fresh groceries into one box, the canned goods into another, and the turkey all by itself.

"Why don't we make another box with some crayons, books, pencils, a ball, a jumprope, things like that for the children to play with over the holiday weekend?" Sally suggests.

"We've spent all our money," I say, "but we could each bring something of our own that is like new. Would that do?"

"There are lots of things I can't use now," says Sally, not in a whiney way. "I can bring the skates I got for my birthday."

"I have an unopened pack of construction paper, all colors, and some scissors," I offer.

"I have an unopened box of note paper. It has pink flowers on it," says Margaret.

"I have a new bottle of hand lotion and I bet Drew has some kind of game or ball." suggests Della.

It is dark by the time we finish. "It is too late to deliver tonight, girls, but James will bring the loaded Packard to school and take you tomorrow. I'll add some fresh flowers to the boxes," directs Mrs. Hunt.

I can hardly wait for the end of school. This has been so much fun I have not thought about the children's choir or anything.

James is waiting for us. We pile in. The boxes are gorgeous. Mrs. Hunt has put a bouquet of chrysanthemums from her garden, yellow and bronze and white in the box with ... what? ... a pumpkin! Oh what a happy day!

We sing "Row, row, row your boat" as we drive. I'm so happy I don't care if I can't carry a tune. I sing anyway and nobody even gives me a look.

Mrs. Williams knows we are coming and she is watching for us. "You are sweet children to do this for me and my family," she says with dignity.

Margaret steps forward. Oh gracious, what tacky thing is she going to say?

"Mrs. Williams, the whole sixth grade had such a happy time preparing a gift for you that you all are the ones that gave us a gift," Margaret says looking straight at her and smiling with her whole face.

Wow! I could never have thought of that to say. Margaret must be maturing!

"Wasn't it the best day?" we ask each other on the way home.

"Margaret, you made a really good chairman," I say.

"Thank you, Eliza. I think everybody was wonderful -- especially Audrey."

We all turn to Audrey, who is seated very straight. "Derrick and I heard today that Aunt Christina was killed in the bombing of Coventry. I didn't tell you right off because I was afraid the news would spoil our day and it was a wonderful day. Aunt Tina would have liked what we did."

Chapter L

CHRISTMAS CAROLS

"Eliza, telephone."

"Hello. Oh, hello, Mr. Huffman. I'm fine, thank you. What is that? I've never done that before. Yes, I bet I could. Yes, I will come to practice. Thank you. Goodbye."

"Momma, Momma! Mr. Huffman wants me to be the narrator of the children's choir. I am to introduce each song and say something about it. I haven't done that before but Mrs. Freeland makes us speak on our feet so much that I'm sure I can! I know how to project my voice and how to make eye contact with the audience. And I'll still be part of the choir! That's the best Christmas present I could have!" I hug and hug Momma.

"Today is the first day that silence is golden," says Gamma coming in to see what all the fuss is about. "There is a three dollar fine for unnecessary honking of the automobile horn, for loud playing of the radio or musical instrument or even disturbance by pets. I hope Mr. Smith next door will keep his parrot quiet. Else he'll make a lot of cash for the city. Eliza, am I hearing that you are to be part of the children's choir?"

"Oh, yes, Gamma, and I won't be fined for singing too loud or off key! I'll be speaking!"

"It is hard to believe that December is here. There is always so much to do. Lourrine is going to her family in Mississippi for several months, so I must make some arrangements about the laundry. That is too much for Minerva with her cooking and cleaning," says Momma taking out her list.

"We could use Loeb's damp wash. Mrs. Broadus says they use it and it costs less than any home method and is far more sanitary. And you know how she watches every penny," suggests Gamma. "And for a small additional charge, you can have the shirts and flat work finished. Why don't you let that be my contribution?"

"Gamma, Gardner would really appreciate that. And I do, too," says Momma as she gives her momma a hug. "Thank you."

"Look, here in today's paper. The first West Tennessee selectees for the new draft army. They are at Ft. Oglethorpe, Georgia, and are in for a year's service. Tennessee will have a heavier quota in January. I'm so grateful Bill is only 15," Momma says.

"Also," she continues, "it is time to get off our Christmas box to cousin Betty and cousin Bobby and Uncle Hoss and Aunt Laurie. Good shopper Eliza, have you any suggestions?"

"Oh, yes, Momma, Sally and I have been studying all the ads."

"Oh wow!" says Bill, "what a thrill!"

"Oh hush up," I almost laugh. "You like it when you get a special gift. Momma, Gerbers has 12-ounce glasses with a monogram, six for a dollar. And a man's fitted travel case, black or brown genuine leather, with a zipper fastener. It has a hair brush, comb, mirror, nail file, razor box, toothbrush holder and lotion bottle. All for a dollar."

"That does sound nice," admits Bill. "But all this talk about shopping drives me silly. I just go to town one day and do it all. I don't make lists."

"I bet your money doesn't go as far."

"Maybe not, but think of all the extra time I have!" Bill likes the last word.

"I have something to say about shopping," Poppa comes in. "Eliza, I think anybody who can narrate a choral group can certainly accompany me on a shopping spree for her mother. Shall we shop and then have lunch at The Peabody?"

"Oh, Poppa, yes! What day? It will have to be a Saturday."

"And you are willing to give up your movie to shop with your ole Poppa? That is heartwarming to hear," he chuckles. "How about the 14th?"

Chapter LI

SHOPPING WITH POPPA

The Christmas tree stands in a bucket of water on the back porch. Minerva's toll house cookies with extra pecans that I helped shell are made and under lock and key. Gamma's cards to friends and family in Alabama and Rhode Island are written and stacked on the mail table. Certain special ones have a handkerchief enclosed. Sally and I have made our decisions. The movie party was such fun last year, we are doing an encore, after Christmas, but while the trees are still up. Audrey and Derrick will talk to their parents either on Christmas Eve or the day after Christmas, which Audrey says is "Boxing Day."

Audrey says she doesn't know about Santa Claus. They have Father Christmas. And eggnog? She's never heard of that, but plum pudding! "It is gorgeous! It is divine!" she says.

I would be homesick three thousand miles from home at Christmas time, but Audrey says, "I miss my parents, but it is wonderful over here."

Derrick told Bill that for the last few holiday seasons, before coming to the U.S., they stayed at his parents' other home on the Isle of Jersey. One time his nine-and-a-half foot canoe carried him five miles into the English Chanel. "It's a great sport!" he said. No wonder he and Bill get along so well.

Poppa has gone early to the office, even though it is Saturday. I am to meet him there at 11 o'clock. I wear my Sunday coat, gray with a wine velvet collar and a matching hat, and my good black patent leather shoes, and white angora gloves. My seven cent bus fare is tucked safely inside one glove.

The fun begins with the two-and-a-half block walk to the bus. The sky is clear and blue with a few white clouds. Leaves are gone and trees are bare. What is that we memorized with Mrs. Hughes? "The trees are black lace against the winter sky." They are, they really are! And is it cold! The wind bites my cheeks and my eyes "cry." My best, heaviest coat and I am shivering. I hope the bus is right on time.

The bus is warm and I choose a window seat. I love to ride the bus to town, especially if I am not going to the dentist. I know all the stops. This one coming up is by the clinic. Always lots of people there. Mostly colored people. Many get on and move to the back. Some have to stand. The vacant seats up front are for white people only. That's the way it is. Maybe some will get off soon and no one will have to stand long. The bus turns onto Main Street. Oh! Beautiful! Red and green tinsel garlands hang across the street as far as I can see. And the department store windows have big Santa's and electric trains and dolls and sleds! Oh, what if it would snow? I pull the cord for my stop, right in front of the pink and blue candy store, in the lobby of Poppa's office building. "Tenth floor, please," I say to the man running the elevator. "I'm going shopping with my poppa."

"I know your poppa; he is a fine man."

I enter two large swinging doors. A secretary at the door smiles and says, "Eliza, Mr. Horton is waiting for you. He says to go right in."

I hurry across the thick, smooth wine carpet that must be vacuumed every day because it shows foot prints. Poppa's office has his name on the door. He opens the door before I have a chance to knock. "I'm not late, Poppa."

"No, you are exactly on the dot. I am just eager. Do you think it is going to snow?" as he puts on his overcoat and gets his hat and white silk muffler. "Did you get any clues as to what your momma would like?"

"Yes, Poppa. She says that she needs a new black leather handbag."

"Then we'll go to Gerber's first" and Poppa reaches to punch the buzzer for the elevator, but it is right there, waiting. "Good morning again, Captain," Poppa says to the elevator man, "my daughter and I are going out on the town."

"Yessir, Mr. Horton. A mighty fine young lady she is too."

It is a cold walk to Gerber's, and the sky has turned grey. The warm air of the store feels so good. "Hello, Mr. Horton."

"Good day to you, Mr. McPhillips. This is my daughter, Eliza."

"Hello, young lady. Taking daddy out shopping?"

"Hello, Mr. McPhillips. Yes, sir. We are shopping for Momma."

Christmas carols fill the store. "Silent night, holy night." I will never stop loving Christmas carols. Red velvet bows and evergreen branches and white twinkling lights decorate the store and people smile and look top-heavy with their patchwork of wrapped packages. I tingle all over.

"I believe the handbags are on the main floor," and Poppa goes right to the counter.

"Yes, sir?" asks a smiling clerk.

"I would like to see a black leather handbag for a petite lady."

"For evening or for daytime?"

Poppa looks at me. "For daytime," I answer.

The clerk opens the glass case and brings out three. "These are all lovely bags, sir."

"Which one do you think, Eliza?"

"They are all pretty, Poppa, but I like the one with the gold clasp."

"That will be the one then,"

"It is a handsome bag. Let me show you: it is lined in leather and has a mirror and comb and chained coin purse."

"Oh, Poppa, that is beautiful, but," I pull on his sleeve.

"What's that?"

I bend his ear to mine. "You haven't asked how much it costs. It may be too much."

"Not for a Christmas present for your mother," he says quietly.

Poppa pulls out bills and pays for the purse and we leave it at the gift wrap counter. "Now, let us go to Ladies Lingerie. Your mother always likes something pretty. We are having our Christmas Afternoon Open House again this year and ...."

"May I help you, sir?"

"Yes, please, my daughter and I would like to see a hostess gown for her mother. Something red, I think. Yes, red."

"What size, sir?"

"Petite. The smallest and the reddest and the prettiest you have."

"Let me go look in the back," and the clerk disappears.

"Poppa, that will be expensive. It always is when they go to the back," I whisper.

The clerk emerges with a long red velvet hostess gown that has a small train in the back and sleeves that fall.

"Well, Tootsie, do you think she would like that? Will that be the perfect new gown for the Open House?" Poppa's eyes fill with tears.

"Ohh, Poppa, that is so beautiful. It is the most beautiful I have ever seen."

"We'll take it!"

The robe is wrapped in red foil with a large green satin bow and the purse is wrapped in silver foil with a red satin bow. "Let's leave these at the office before we go to lunch," Poppa leads the way. "Are you having fun?"

"Oh, yes, Poppa. Momma never shops without asking the price."

The walk to the Hotel Peabody is brisk. The skies are heavy. "Snow?"

Poppa looks up. "Might be."

Poppa gives his overcoat and hat to the hatcheck girl and helps me off with mine. "Do you want to wear your hat? It looks very nice with your dress."

I hadn't thought about that. "What do you think, Poppa?"

"Most ladies do keep their hats on when they dine and yours is especially becoming."

I blush with pleasure. I didn't know I looked good in a hat. I'll have to check the mirror.

"Good afternoon, Mr. Horton, we've been watching for you and your daughter."

"Good afternoon, Alonzo. Thank you. This is my daughter, Eliza."

"Welcome, little miss. Welcome to The Peabody."

"Thank you, Alonzo. This is my first time to eat lunch here."

"Then we shall see that it is something to remember."

I hear the loveliest music. A harp! And violins! We are seated where we can see the musicians. The table cloth is so snowy white and the napkins huge and starched. Three Christmas Red carnations and florist fern are in a silver vase. Christmas carols on a harp! Music swirls around my head.

"What would you like to eat, Eliza? Or would you like for me to suggest something? I don't believe they have peanut butter and jelly," Poppa teases.

The menu is almost too large to hold. "Yes, Poppa, please help me but you know I don't like brussel sprouts or liver," I say quickly to protect myself.

"Their specialty is French onion soup."

"I've never had that. I'll have to tell Renee. Poppa, could I have a white meat turkey sandwich? We never have enough white meat left over for sandwiches." Then I see a cart of at least twelve desserts roll by. Cherry tarts, chocolate eclairs, and a swan! "Poppa, what's that?"

"Looks beautiful, doesn't it? The dessert cart at the Peabody is a work of art! If you are still hungry after your soup and sandwich, you may choose one."

I want to say that I would rather skip the onion soup and be sure I have room, but I don't.

The soup is thick with onions and lots of grated parmesan cheese on the top. It is different and I'm glad I can say that I've had The Peabody's specialty. A little goes a long way. The turkey sandwich is delicious, white bread with the crusts cut off and Durkees dressing. And I am too full for dessert. "Why can't we have dessert first? When would it taste the best?" I ask, knowing Poppa will give the wholesome food lecture.

"That does seem backwards, doesn't it? Would you like to take one home and have it tonight first before supper?"

I can't believe my ears! "Oh, Poppa, yes!! Could I? But could we take one home to everybody?" I'm thinking if I had to share with five people there wouldn't be a bite left.

"That's very thoughtful, Eliza. Let's do! Of course, Minerva might have her feelings hurt if we don't eat her good supper," Poppa says.

"I bet we'll still be hungry, unless we have something ooky, then I'm not hungry anyway."

The waiter packs six works of art from the dessert cart. The angelic sounds of harp and Christmas carols follow us to the blast of cold air as Poppa opens the heavy outside door. We look up. A flake! Another! And another! It's snowing!! By the time we reach Poppa's office, the flakes are as thick as popcorn balls. The drive home is slow and cautious, but drivers are smiling!

Momma has the fire going. And hot cocoa!

"And we brought you all surprises! And it is snowing! The whole world is white and wrapped in the heart of Christmas."

Chapter LII

NO CHRISTMAS TRUCE

"I just knew there would be a truce on Christmas Day, the way it was last year. Weren't we all counting on it?"

"Pope Pius issued a plea for a Christmas truce, but his plea was ignored", says Gamma sadly.

"There are some things to be happy about though," adds Momma. "Forty-two hundred needy families received large food baskets. And all our boys that were called up in the first selective service are home for Christmas. And I am just so thankful that Bill is only 15."

"Almost 16. I'll be driving soon," Bill is counting the days. "The guys in the service say they learn a lot. The next call will be for ages 18 to 21."

"What did you say, Bill? I didn't see that." Momma's voice is stricken. "Eighteen is so young."

"It was in Sunday's paper, Momma," Bill answers.

"I guess I never really saw Sunday's paper."

"You were busy with your Altar Guild work and then making eggnog," says Poppa as he puts his arm around her. "Bill has two and a half years before he is 18."

"Eliza, Catherine on the phone."

"Audrey just talked to her parents. Why don't you come over and see our tree?"

"I'd love to."

Catherine's tree reaches the ceiling in the library. It is in front of the big window and I could see the lights as we drove up.

"It's huge! And you have lights on your gate! It is beautiful! Hey, Audrey. Could you hear your parents?"

"Yes. I could. We didn't really say much. Just "How are you?" and "I'm fine" and "It's good to hear your voice." But I heard them and they do sound fine, really they do," Audrey says quietly. "Derrick asked about the food situation. Father said the situation was serious but not desperate."

"Oh."

"Yes, I did read in your paper that the food situation was as bleak as in the bleakest days of World War I. The farmers are being exhorted to increase production, but, of course, most of the farmers have gone to war. Conscientious objectors have been sent to farm. You know, those men who have a religious objection to fighting. Any additional labor will have to be women."

"Women?"

"Yes. King George gives his Christmas message tomorrow. Will it be on your wireless?"

"I'm certain it will, Audrey," says Mrs. Hunt as she enters the library. "Your King is such a fine man. Did I tell you that our local British War Relief Society has been raising money for your cause through the sale of the Christmas cards bearing his last Christmas message to his subjects? It is full of faith. Let me go find one and read it to you."

Mrs. Hunt returns promptly. "Here it is:

I said to a man who stood at the gate of the year. 'Give me a light that I may tread safely into the unknown.' And he replied,'Go out into the darkness and put your hand into the hand of God. That shall be to you better than a light and safer than a known way.'

With all good wishes
for a
Merry Christmas
and a
Happy New Year.

Your King is a person to be proud of."

Chapter LIII

LOOKING AHEAD IN 1941

"Happy 1941!" says Momma as she gives me a New Year's hug. "Did you hear the New Year come in?"

"We did. Lawrence's mother had cocoa and oatmeal cookies for us at midnight. I'm sure there is no New Year's truce," I say.

"There is! In God's own way. Bad weather prevented the Luftwaffe's flying and delivering their New Year's 'greeting' of bombs," Momma smiles. "I also heard on the radio that the besieged people of London welcomed in 1941 with all the gaiety they could muster. Underground cafes were crowded with merry-makers deep below the blacked-out streets. Edward R. Murrow said he could hear the strains of 'Auld Lang Syne.'"

"It is predicted that 1941 will be the best business year in history," reads Poppa. "We need the same thing to be true for the farmers."

"Wrap up if you go out, Bill. One person in six has the flu," Momma worries.

"But it's not like that serious epidemic in 1918," comments Gamma. "And did you see where the Ice Parade of 1941 will be in the Skyway at the Hotel Peabody. They will have real ice! I cannot imagine it!"

"Is it expensive to go? How much are the tickets?"

"The announcement didn't say, so they must be very expensive!"

"Is anyone making New Year's resolutions?" asks Gamma. "I see Mr. Roosevelt is.

"He needs to," retorts Poppa. "And to think we have four more years of FDR."

"I don't remember another president. He was elected when I was three years old," I say. "And I go to confirmation class this year."

"And I will get my driver's license," adds Bill.

"I hope we will have a new bridge over the Mississippi. The Harahan Bridge is overloaded with traffic," Poppa says.

"Eliza, this letter came for you yesterday afternoon, after you had gone to Lawrence's. Looks like Aunt Lucy's handwriting."

"Oh, I bet she's answering mine. In my Christmas thank-you letter, I told her about Audrey and Derrick," I say as I tear open the envelope.

Dear Eliza,

I'm glad you didn't already have <u>Little Women</u>. I read it with your mother when she was your age.

Yes, we are snowed in, but spring will come and so will summer. I wonder if you and Bill would like to visit me this summer? Bill could work with Jake in The Orchard and sail in his spare time.

You could help me in my garden and we could read and play 'Sympathy.'

I also was wondering if you might like to bring Audrey and Derrick. I would love to have them. And maybe Mr. and Mrs. Hunt could use a break in their schedule. What do you think? Ask your Momma.

Yes, New England is much closer to the war than Tennessee is. We even have air-spotters now. Twelve thousand! We volunteer at almost 700 observation posts. We won't be caught napping if an invasion comes.

With love from Aunt Lucy

"Oh, Momma, what do you think?"

"I think Aunt Lucy is lovely to invite you all. And I hear her saying that she would enjoy the company. We'll see," say Momma.

"Is that the 'see' part of 'wait and see'? I ask.

"Yes, I suppose it is. I'll talk to your Poppa. I don't need to ask you, Bill. I know you want to go. Would you like to have Audrey and Derrick go with you? You would be sharing Aunt Lucy, you realize?"

"That's true," I agree. "But I like Audrey a lot, and I know Aunt Lucy would love to have a house full of folks. When would we go?" And, I think to myself, if I've still got the stupid Slam Book when summer comes, I can just take it in the bottom of my suitcase and burn it in the grate one cool night. Surely the train won't be stopped a second time.

"Probably at the hottest part of the summer here. Like July and maybe August," Momma never forgets the danger of infantile paralysis.

"Momma, you have a good idea. Derrick has missed being near the sea, and I like him. He has made a good impression at Central High. Both of them are brave and uncomplaining. And you are right, you know I want to go. Gamma, would you be going?"

"I always seize the opportunity to escape the Memphis heat, but I was there the last two summers and I don't want to wear out my welcome. Anyway, Aunt Lucy invited you all. I don't believe she said anything about me."

I look again at my letter. "Well, she didn't actually, Gamma, but I bet she was just 'testing the waters' to see if we would like to come."

"Yankees always mean exactly what they say," Gamma's voice has a little touch of a tone in it. "And I think the newlyweds don't need too many house guests this year. Also, you and Bill are experienced enough to travel together on the train with Audrey and Derrick. Maybe I'll go see Sister in New Orleans."

"We need a conference with all the people involved," pronounces Poppa, "And my pocketbook."

Chapter LIV

TWO SAILORS ON THE TRAIN

"Trains are always crowded," Bill observes, "but this summer, more than ever, and look at all the servicemen. Derrick, let's go talk to those two sailors."

"Audrey, I don't see how you can write when the train is moving. Is that a letter to your parents?"

"No, actually, I am writing in my journal. I like to record what I see and do; so I can remember when I get home. When we arrived on the train, I was so tired and excited that I don't remember what I saw. Your country is so big!"

"Do you think much about when you are going home?" I ask.

"No, not really. I do follow the war news very closely though."

"I haven't read the papers that much since school has been out, although I'm sure Mrs. Freeland will send us an August assignment. What have you read?"

"That the Nazis are sinking ships faster than we can build them," sighs Audrey, "but your president has signed the Lend-Lease Bill. That will help. And there are Americans who fly for Britain in the R. A. F.: #71 ... The Eagle Squadron. They come to England as experienced fliers, but are also given six months' training before being sent into action."

Bill and Derrick and the two sailors join us. "Yep, and those in the Eagle Squadron are from the north and south, east and west, and from all walks of life," Bill adds. "These two guys, Roy and George, are stationed on our new air-craft carrier, The Enterprise. Tell the girls what you were telling us."

"Hi," says Roy, "Now what I am telling you is no secret. There were pictures of her in *Life*. The Enterprise is a brand-new battle device. She's a sea-going landing field!"

"And she carries 81 planes," adds George.

"Are you a pilot?" I ask. "That's what Bill wants to be."

"No. I'm one who looks after the planes. The planes come in for a landing and have to be caught by arresting gear. That's a series of steel cables stretched across the flight deck. There is a hook on the outside of each plane."

"So the planes won't keep on going into into the ocean? The carrier does seem like a small place to try to land," I say. "Can some planes take off and others land at the same time?"

"Yes."

"Wow! Where are they kept when all 81 are on the carrier?"

"On the hangar deck, one deck below. They ride down on elevators and I bet you don't know that their wings fold up and the planes actually snuggle together when we put them to bed," George seems to like what he does.

"Have you sailed to different countries? Do you really 'join the Navy and see the world'?" I ask. George surely is easy to talk to.

"We've been mainly in the Pacific. We've put in at Guam, which the United States fortified this spring. And Australia, the land of sheep."

"And mines and timber," adds Roy. "I am impressed with that country. She has only seven million people, but she is out-producing England and the U.S."

"I say, are you certain?" asks Derrick.

"Yes, Australia has done the best job of all democracies of re-arming in a hurry without waste or fuss or unnecessary delay," answers Roy.

"Is she out-producing Spitfires and Hurricanes?" Derrick cannot believe his ears.

"And the U.S. is making Packard engines for the Spitfires and Hurricanes," Bill adds.

"Well, no. The planes Australia makes are training planes. But it's just that she used to buy all her manufactured goods from England and now she has quietly created her own industrial plant."

"That is impressive. The only explanation could be strong leadership," observes Derrick. "Who is responsible?"

"You are right, Derrick. So much depends on leadership. We were told that the credit goes especially to the Director General of Munitions, a Mr. Essing Lewis."

"Do many planes crash?" I ask.

"Many? No. Some, yes."

"The R.A.F. shot down 3,500 German planes in 1940," Audrey adds. "We lost 1,050, but 400 pilots were saved."

"But planes crash that aren't being shot at," I add. "Gamma said that the first 17 months of our having air passenger service, there was not a single crash. Of course, I don't believe Gamma would take a plane anyhow, but then there were five crashes in seven months beginning last August. Now, I know she will never fly."

"Why did they crash?"

"Mostly weather," answers Bill, "but sometimes human stupidity. One time, a bolt of lightning hit in the plane's path; pressure and sound waves stunned both pilots and the plane dived into the ground. All 25 aboard were killed. Another time, outside

Salt Lake City, a plane crashed in a snowstorm, but that did not have to be. The radio range had been knocked out for three hours and not one of the four observers reported it and all ten aboard were killed."

"I wonder how those observers can stand it," I murmur. "Do you really want to fly?"

"I sure do."

"Do you want to fly planes that land on a carrier?"

"Maybe."

"There wouldn't be many pilots with only 81 planes."

"Well, the U.S. now has six carriers and a dozen more being built."

"Oh. Are carriers in the middle of a battle?"

Roy answers, "No, in combat, she would be stationed well behind the main line of battle, but her planes would be well out in advance. The fighters trying to knock out the enemy's planes and then her bombers and torpedo planes attacking."

"Oh. There are several kinds of planes on the carrier?"

"Right."

I think Roy is nice too. "How does the carrier keep from getting attacked by enemy planes? Or am I asking a secret? I know we are supposed to 'button our lips,'" I smile at Roy.

"This is all general knowledge. The carrier is only lightly armed and relies on speed for her protection and on a screen of warships." Roy really knows a lot.

"Does Britain have any carriers?" asks Audrey.

"Yes," Derrick answers his sister, "She has eight."

"And Japan?"

"She probably has seven," answers George.

"Why don't we eat while we talk?"

"Good idea." And we lurch and lunge our way through the heavy doors and the crowds. And we have to stand in line for a table.

"I'm starved!"

"I could eat a horse."

"Some people are eating horses."

Suddenly everyone is quiet.

"I read that the people of unoccupied France are living on one-half pound of food a day," Audrey is almost reciting.

"I don't know how much food that is," I confess.

"The article said that the average American eats four pounds a day," Audrey answers.

"Oh? That's a big difference. I guess I have never been really hungry. I wonder about the people who have been taken prisoner."

"Your *Life* magazine said there were 38,000 Britons living in Germany as prisoners. I don't know what prisoners get fed."

"They are supposed to get what other people get, but I bet they don't."

"Belgians are starving. I read that. More than eight million. I cannot even comprehend that many people. They are looking to the United States for food," Audrey continues. "The children are below normal in weight and stature, and they are listless and pale with dark circles under their eyes. They are so listless that they cannot stay awake in class."

"Well, that happens to me sometime," Bill laughs as we move up a little in line.

Audrey doesn't laugh. "They throw up, but they have nothing to throw up but potato peels."

"Audrey, we are going to eat. Tell us more later," Derrick presses her arm gently.

"All right. This is the last thing. Their daily diet is four slices of bread, one potato and 2 lumps of sugar. The doctors say that bodies and brains have been damaged forever. Now, I'm through. Bill, are you going to order soup?" Audrey is herself again.

—⁓—

"That's Aunt Lucy, over there in the big straw hat!" She and James hurry towards us.

Aunt Lucy gathers us all at once into her arms, even Bill and Derrick, who seem surprised but not unwilling. We shake hands with James and somehow get all our luggage and ourselves into the still-shiny black Buick.

"The stone walls are standing," I observe joyfully.

"And smell the sea!" Derrick is grinning.

"The Orchard is not actually on the water, Derrick, but we are not too far away," explains Aunt Lucy, "you and Bill can sail any day that the weather permits, after you have done your chores, of course."

"Miss Conway, your home reminds me more of an English cottage than any I have seen since we came to America," Audrey walks slowly around the sitting room letting her fingers touch the blue and white teapot and the china figures of dogs. "And you have roses!" Audrey sniffs the bouquet of yellow roses in a crystal pitcher. The sunlight hits the crystal just right and makes a brief rainbow. Audrey bursts into smiles and says, "Oh, how I love the sunlight! I think Britons never get enough. Miss Conway, what a heavenly place!"

Aunt Lucy looks out the window at Bill and Derrick inspecting the apple orchard, at Brandy and Cocoa close on their heels, at James wiping the station dust from the Buick, at Rose bringing in a basket of vegetables, and turns to us, seeing what she sees. "It is a heavenly place."

She grabs our hands. "Come! I'll show you my official spotter hat, before I burst with joy!"

Chapter LV

THE SAME, BUT NOT THE SAME

"Audrey, you will love camp. And they are the nicest girls. Frances, Anna, Caroline, and Elizabeth."

"I'll try to remember their names," says Audrey.

"You can, easy; they spell F-A-C-E," I reveal, "that's how I remembered the first time. Golly, that was two summers ago!"

The surf still pounds the rocks at Warren's Point and the white foam leaps into the air. But I'm not afraid of the salt water's stinging my eyes or the uneven sandy bottom. I might even jump off one of the rocks!

"Audrey, is it like your sea at home? It is the same ocean, you know, but does it look the same?" asks Frances, who hasn't changed into her bathing suit.

"We have rocky coasts, too, Frances, but now our seashores are not so lovely. They're all lined with barbed wire and dotted with pill boxes against a possible invasion. But Mother wrote that since Hitler invaded Russia the end of June and is busy on that front, he doesn't have time or planes to bother England right now. So, barbed wire or not, people are at the shore on holiday, getting any sun they can. I love your sunshine. Aren't you going to bathe?" asks Audrey.

"No, not today. You know," answers Frances. "Neither is Anna."

"Oh, I see," nods Audrey.

"Why?" I ask, but as soon as the word escapes me, I know. How can I be so dumb. I feel my face getting red.

"You don't know, Eliza? I thought southern girls knew all there was to know," Frances says not unkindly. "Hasn't your mother told you about the curse? Or I guess you haven't started yet?"

"No, I mean, yes. Yes, I mean, no. Yes, Momma has told me; no, I haven't started yet," I stammer. "But I know you can't go swimming and that you are not supposed to question anybody who says she can't go swimming. I think that would be embarrassing if you were with boys and girls. Then, they would know."

"Well, Anna says a boy can tell just by looking at you," reveals the more mature Frances, "but I'm not sure how."

"Could you tell you were going to start?" I ask. "Or did you just start and not know until you went to the bathroom? What I really mean, is did you bleed on your skirt?"

"I know what you mean, Eliza. I've been looking at the back of my skirt every time I got up from my desk for the last year," confides Frances. "I was really relieved when I started. At least, I kind of know when to look for it."

"All the girls at school take a Kotex and a belt in the zipper part of their notebook, just in case," I reveal. "But Momma said she was late starting and I probably would be too. Thirteen or maybe fourteen."

Audrey doesn't say anything. Maybe she misses her mother. I hadn't thought about that. I wonder if English girls start at the same time as American girls. Momma said something about girls who live in the tropics mature earlier. England is further north. I wish Audrey would say something. I know she wears a bra; I've seen the pair of straps through her gym shirt. I don't need a bra, but I wish I could have one just so I would have straps to show through my gym shirt. I know if I were to ask Momma for one, she would say, "Eliza, you don't need one; I didn't when I was your age." I think all the girls at camp wear one and I bet they have all started too. I wonder if they shave their legs. If they shave their legs, then they must shave under their arms too. And if they have hair under their arms, they they got hair in that other place too. I look down at my flat bathing suit. I feel terribly left out.

"Eliza!" comes a voice. "It's so nice to have you back. After we dry off, come tell us about your adventure on the train last summer. We all admired your traveling alone and your kindness to your friend," welcomes my favorite counselor. She hands me a towel. "There are lots of ways of growing up. Some people get taller or bloom in other ways in their bodies; some people grow in their hearts first."

Chapter LVII

GETTING RID OF THE SLAM BOOK, ONCE AND FOR ALL

"**A**unt Lucy, when are we going to have a fire in the grate?"

"As soon as we have a very cool night, I suppose," answers Aunt Lucy, looking up from her typewriter. "I do remember how intrigued you were with a fire in July."

"Yes. Well, it's August and we haven't had one. Could we have one tonight?"

"We won't need one tonight, Eliza. You know, a fire is not appealing unless there's a chill in the air," reasons Aunt Lucy.

"Couldn't we have one anyway? Please?"

"What's up, Eliza?" Aunt Lucy looks at me quizzically. "Something's up."

"I need to burn something. That's all, Aunt Lucy."

"The plot thickens," smiles Aunt Lucy as she gets up from her desk chair and takes my hands in hers and leads me to love seat covered in chintz of pink roses. "Tell me," she says gently, "that is, if you want to, what you need to destroy."

"I do want to tell you. It's been bothering me for such a long time," I say in a whispered voice. And I tell her about finding the Slam Book in my desk and how anyone found with one would be punished. And worst of all, what was written in it.

"What a big problem to carry around," responds Aunt Lucy.

"I was going to burn the book last summer and then ... you know I got sent back home. I don't think about it every day the way I used to."

"That's good enough to put in one of my stories," confides Aunt Lucy.

"Really?" I question.

"Indeed. Only I probably wouldn't have the protagonist burn it."

"You wouldn't? Why not? I thought about flushing the pages down the toilet ... but, you know, that gets complicated. I would still have been left with the red backing. I thought burning was a good way," I say.

"Hitler burns books he's afraid of. But does that destroy the ideas?"

"No. But I don't see how that applies to a Slam Book," I am trying to follow, but just talking to Aunt Lucy makes me feel better.

"First, would that solve the problem? What I mean is, is just getting rid of the book the problem?"

"Part of it. I couldn't get caught with it. I did think about writing something mean on Margaret's page and putting it in her desk, but I was afraid I would be seen ... and ... I don't know."

"You obviously think Margaret put it in your desk?"

"Yes. I'm sure. I think."

"You think she wrote all those comments and disguised her handwriting?" asks Aunt Lucy.

"That's what Catherine thought," I reply. "It hurt my feelings so bad." A tear starts down. My nose burns.

"So even if you burn the book, the hurt feelings will still be there?"

"I guess so. At least, I know that it's probably just Margaret who doesn't like me. But if she made up that she can make up other stuff. How can I get back at her?"

"One thing at a time. First, everybody is not going to have

everybody as a best friend. There will always be some people that we like better than others. Right?" Aunt Lucy sounds very practical.

"Jesus says we are to love everybody ... even our enemies, but I don't see how that is possible. How can I love Margaret after she was so mean? How can Audrey love the Germans? That doesn't make sense," I puzzle.

"The verb "to love" has several meanings. We often think a warm, fuzzy feeling is the meaning of love. But that is just a feeling. I think Jesus meant for us to think with our minds that we will consciously try to desire what is good for that person," Aunt Lucy says slowly.

"Like what?"

"Well, probably Margaret wrote those unkind things because she was sad or unhappy or jealous?"

"Well, Barbara did say that she had been at Miss Meriwether's since kindergarten and so had her mother and that her sister had been princess. But she still shouldn't have been so awful to me. What if I had been caught with the book?"

"Eliza, do you know I believe Miss Meriwether would have listened to your story. Did you ever think of that?"

"No. Why would she believe a new girl?"

"It is the business of headmistresses to believe in their girls," explains Aunt Lucy, "and to help them sort out things."

"The only way Margaret won't start some more trouble is to make her like me and I can't do that. I don't even know if I want to. Yes, I do too. It would be nice if she liked me."

"Has there been any time that you liked Margaret?" asks Aunt Lucy.

"Well, yes. She did a wonderful job as chairman of our Junior Red Cross Thanksgiving basket for a poor family. And she said just the right thing to the mother," I remember. "I even told me her so."

"Could you wish for her to have more opportunities like that?" asks Aunt Lucy.

"Sure. That's easy. She was like a different person."

"That's one way you 'love your enemies,'" reveals Aunt Lucy. "Wish for something good for them. You could even help by, say, nominating her for a job at school?"

"Okay. But what do I do with the book?"

"It doesn't matter now. Just throw it in my trash basket. And don't look back. As Grandfather Comstock used to say, "Never stumble over something behind you."

Chapter LVII

SOMETIMES STORMY DAYS ARE THE BRIGHTEST

"No camp today? A big blow, maybe all day? See you tomorrow then. Goodbye." I hang up and gloomily report to Aunt Lucy and Audrey.

"That's good news. Now I've got help with my chores all day," chuckles Aunt Lucy. "Here is my list," and Aunt Lucy starts writing.

"You are making that up right now, Aunt Lucy. You don't really have a list." I can't help laughing at Aunt Lucy.

"I may be just be writing it now, but it's in my head, always in my head:

1.) wash and brush Brandy and Cocoa

2.) help Rose make two apple pies

3.) each person read one news item

4.) paste pictures in the photo album (in chronological order)

5.) invent a three handed 'Sympathy'

6.) each person write home

7.) help Aunt Lucy dust the books in the sitting room

8.) each person chooses a dusted book and read for an hour

Now, that should do it!" Aunt Lucy looks pleased with herself. "Bill and Derrick can wash Brandy and you and Audrey can bathe Cocoa."

"It's raining, Aunt Lucy."

"Improvise, my dears, improvise," and Aunt Lucy heads for her typewriter.

"We could bathe Cocoa in the cellar," suggests Audrey.

"No, it's so gloomy down there," I say, but I mean 'spidery'. "Why don't we just bathe him outside? And let the rain rinse him off."

"Right. Let's get our sou'westers. Hurry, I don't want the guys to copy us."

Bill and Derrick brave the cellar and are rubbing Brandy dry in front of the sitting room fire when we drip in, chilled to the bone.

"So much for your improvisation," laughs Bill. "If you weren't afraid of spiders, all three of you would be dry."

"True," I concede, "but I didn't have to lay the fire!"

"You will, sister-dear, you will. And by then, the wood will be soaked. Unless you are willing to get dry logs from the cellar. Heh, heh, heh," Bill rubs his hands together, chuckling.

"Apple peeling time," calls Rose. "Miss Lucy had a good idea. You young 'uns eat a pie so fast, you ought to know the time it takes to make one."

"Cooking is woman's work," says Derrick. "We picked the apples."

"Miss Lucy says that anyone who likes to eat should know how to cook," and Rose hands us each a bowl of apples and a paring knife.

"If you get the peel off all in one piece, you can throw the peel over your shoulder and whatever letter it makes is the initial of the one you will marry," I say.

"Marry? That's all girls ever think about," says Bill. "There is a conspiracy against us men, Derrick."

"You like girls. I bet the first thing you do when you get your driver's license is take Connie Coleman out," I tease. "And I bet you'll take her to the Pig 'n Whistle and park in the back under the trees."

"You're too young to know about The Pig," laughs Bill and

changes the subject, "We're ready, Rose. That wasn't so hard."

Rolling the crust is a little tricky, but we do it! The cinnamon and apple aroma drifts into the sitting room. Bill's fire needs another log.

"Your turn, sister-dear. Which will it be, rain-soaked wood that will do nothing but smoke, or a venture into the den of spiders?"

"Audrey, come with me and bring something to swat with," I can't hide the shiver that runs all through me. "I'll get a flashlight from Aunt Lucy." I want her to know where we are in case we are both bitten by black widows and swoon to the cellar floor.

The cellar steps are short. We shine the light all around. "There's the wood-pile. Is it crawling with things?"

"No, Eliza. Let's play that it's not. And show those boys that we aren't scaredy-cats." Audrey is cool.

"You're right, Audrey. What if bombs were dropping on us? Or what if we were prisoners in an enemy camp? From this moment on, I am brave," I vow and walk straight over to the logs and hold out my arms, "Load me up!"

Audrey does just that and holds the flashlight and opens the door.

"Well, look at her!" says Bill.

"We'll get another load or two," I say casually.

"What's behind those half-doors?" asks Audrey on our third trip down. Our eyes have grown accustomed to the semi-light.

"Probably stuff that's too good to throw away, but Aunt Lucy isn't using anymore. Want to look?"

We shine the light and push the swinging doors. Chests, rocking chair-minus-a-rocker, an old-fashioned lamp painted with roses.

"That looks like an oil lamp," observes Audrey. "Isn't it quaint with the roses? Do you suppose Miss Conway would mind if I took it upstairs?"

"I don't think so, but we might ask first."

"So, Eliza, you've been exploring in the darkened dungeon. Life is more of an adventure when we conquer our fears, isn't it?" Aunt Lucy gives me such a tight hug I can't breathe. "That lamp was in Grandfather's house in Providence. I brought it with me because I like the roses and the satin glass. Meant to have it wired, but never did. By all means, bring it up. With the way the storm is going we may need an oil lamp."

"What's next on our list? Does it say anything about lunch? And apple pie?" asks Bill, who has found some paraffin oil for the lamp, just in case.

"Aunt Lucy, can't we have the pie first? Dessert always tastes better first. And it smells so good."

"Eliza, a truer word was never spoken. Fresh hot apple pie from the oven with a hunk of sharp cheddar cheese and a roaring fire. Call Rose and James and Jake. See if they want to party with us."

"This is more fun than camp, Aunt Lucy."

"We make our own fun, Eliza. Just remember if you have what looks like a dark, disappointing day ahead, just make yourself a list," advises Aunt Lucy.

"How does a list do it?" I question.

"That's just the beginning. It helps to get your thoughts on paper. Always put a thing or two that needs doing, that you have been putting off. Always put a fun thing or two."

"I still don't see how that turns a dark day into a bright one."

"It's simply doing the first thing. Let me ask you: what was fun?"

"Well, it was fun to bathe Cocoa, even in the rain. Audrey and I laughed and laughed. And it was fun for us to try to peel the apples. And it was a good feeling to get over the spiders. I don't know, Aunt Lucy. It was all fun."

"It would not have been quite as much fun by yourself."

"Oh. I guess not," I say, "But, Aunt Lucy, you have fun and you are by yourself." Oh, that's not how I meant to say it. I spoke without thinking.

"Living by myself makes me appreciate other's company even more," Aunt Lucy says easily. "I have Brandy and Cocoa. I have Rose and James and Jake. I have my apple trees and my roses. I have the four of you this summer. And I have my typewriter. And I have God who gave me the good sense to make the most of every day."

All eight of us are seated around the kitchen table. "Tell me something you've read. Derrick, you first?"

"I did read that the German army is headed for Moscow. I don't like the Communists. But Mr. Churchill said that anybody that fights Hitler is on Britain's side. But that was strange to have signed a treaty with Russia and then attack her."

"Well, that gives our country and your country more time to arm ourselves," adds Bill.

"You talk as though we are at war, and we're not, are we?" I ask.

"No. And some people still believe America should not get involved with Europe. The bill just passed to lower the selective service age to 18, but it passed by only one vote," continues Bill.

"Boys and girls, you made good pies," praises Rose. "I guess I'm not needed in the kitchen anymore."

"Nobody cooks like you, Rose!"

"Well, I've scarcely got any pots and pans left to cook in. Miss Lucy has given most of them to the aluminum drive."

"An airplane is 90% aluminum," explains Aunt Lucy.

"We'll manage, Miss Lucy. My sister, Bridgette's, boy has been sent to Greenland. I think they are building an Army and Air base there."

"I hope Mr. Churchill and Mr. Roosevelt did not have storms

like this when they met last week off the coast of Maine."

"Can you imagine all the planning that went on to assure that meeting?" muses Aunt Lucy.

"I bet they made lots of lists, Aunt ..." and crack ... the lights go out!

We all know where candles are and soon they are stationed around the sitting room, on the mantle, in the hall, and in the kitchen.

"It's still daytime but it is almost as black as night. I guess we won't know the difference when night comes," I look out the window. "We need more light to do the things on your list, Aunt Lucy. Do you realize you had eight things on your list?"

"Imagine that!" chuckles Aunt Lucy. "And there were eight of us eating pie around the table!"

"May we use the oil lamp, Miss Conway?" asks Audrey. "Bill has the paraffin."

We troop to the kitchen. "I like satin glass and I love the shape. The round bottom and the round top. With the brass fittings in the middle. It looks like a buxom lady with a tiny waist," laughs Audrey.

I stare at the lamp for a moment. I'm seeing things, "It looks like an 8!" My voice doesn't even sound like my own.

"It does look like an eight! It does!" Everyone is talking at once. "What does it mean?"

"Aunt Lucy, you did say this was your grandfather's lamp?"

Chapter LVIII

PIECES OF EIGHT; PIECES OF JOY

"**A**unt Lucy," Bill's voice has a quiet authority. "have you ever put oil in your lamp?"

"I know I haven't. Come to think of it, Grandfather kept it in his room and I don't remember ever seeing it lighted. The glass is so pretty and the roses painted on it, that I guess, if I thought about it at all, I thought it was too fragile and fine to risk the heat," replies Aunt Lucy. "It should come apart right here to take the oil," and Aunt Lucy deftly removes the top globe. "See, this is the container for the oil. It has a lid."

We are all elbows leaning on the kitchen table trying to see.

"There is a folded paper with writing one it. Here, Eliza, smoothe it out and read it."

The world is brimming with joy just waiting to be discovered....
Capt. Conway

"That sounds like Grandfather. He used to say that every morning. Here, let me see. Is there something in the oil box?" Aunt Lucy turns it upside down and out come ... DIAMONDS!

There is a stunned silence. Aunt Lucy picks up one and then another. We all stand back, not believing our eyes. "Each one is a good size. I would say the smallest one is more than two carats. And there are one, two, three, four ... eight!! EIGHT!! Can you believe it?" Aunt Lucy looks around at us.

"The blue rings were magic," I whisper. "The lamp did look like an 8 and it was there all the time just waiting to be found."

"Like joy ... if we will only look," whispers Aunt Lucy back.

"What are you going to do with them?" asks Bill, "besides have them evaluated and then put them in a safe place."

I know he's thinking what I'm thinking: Aunt Lucy is not the type to bedeck herself with jewels.

"That will take some thought," smiles Aunt Lucy. "I'll make a list."

"What if we hadn't had a storm and the lights gone out?"

"That's not it. The lights go out often and we just use candles. It's because Eliza overcame her fear of spiders and went to the basement," says Bill.

"But Audrey spotted the lamp and asked if we could bring it up," I say.

"But you noticed that it looked like an 8."

"But we would have discovered the treasure when we poured the paraffin."

"Well," laughs Aunt Lucy, "shall we pour the oil and light the wick? As Grandfather used to say, 'Life is not the wick or the candle, it is the burning.' Oh what joy we have discovered!"

"That must mean you have decided what to do with some of the treasure," reasons Bill.

"Yes, indeed. I shall give the largest one to my faithful friend, companion and housekeeper, Rose. She has money worries about her poor mother. And a smaller one to James, for him to buy an automobile of his own. He has never had one and he takes such good care of mine. And one to Jake, a small one to finish paying for his house."

"Aren't you going to use one on yourself, Aunt Lucy?"

"Oh, yes. I shall have all the rest of the hurricane damage repaired. The roof, and the trees we lost and get a new truck," Aunt Lucy responds. "That's all the joy I can handle for one day! What's next on our list?"

Chapter LIX

THE SEVENTH GRADE

"My dears and my darlings, this is your last year in the middle school and my last year to teach you. Next year, you will be in the big study hall and be part of the upper school. It is my job to prepare you. And I am happy to welcome our five new girls. Three new girls from Miss Lee's School of Childhood and two from Idlewild Grammar School, right behind Miss Meriwether's. Both of those schools end with the sixth grade."

Sally gives me a wink. We certainly know where the Idlewild boys' playground is!

"Eliza and Sally, will you be the sponsors for Becky Sue from Idlewild; Renee and Suzanna for Shirley from Idlewild; Della and Mimsy for Lulu from Miss Lee's; Mary Louise and Margaret, for Paula from Miss Lee's, and Helen and Audrey, for Laurie from Miss Lee's. Are there any questions?"

"Yes, Mrs. Freeland. What do the sponsors do?"

"Eliza, Sally and Audrey, you have all been 'new girls'. Can you answer Helen's question?"

"I remember Catherine spoke to me and showed me where to go. By the way, where is Catherine?"

"Catherine is repeating the sixth grade," explains Mrs. Freeland.

A gasp from the class, except Audrey, who knew. "Why?"

"What happened?"

"Catherine did not pass her math and did not do well in French," answers Mrs. Freeland. "Her parents thought it best for her not to go to summer school, but just to drop back a year."

"That is so embarrassing," says Margaret.

"Catherine is not embarrassed," Audrey speaks up. "She agrees with her parents and she says she'll just have twice as many friends, her new grade and her old grade."

"What will she do about ballroom dancing? The sixth grade goes on Friday nights and the seventh on Saturday nights?" asks Margaret.

"I guess she'll go to both," answers Audrey, "if she wants to."

"We could invite the new girls to spend the night and go to the Saturday movies."

"And ask them to serve on committees."

"And tell them about the good lunch on Thursdays."

"And not pull jokes on them until they have been here awhile."

"And not write about them in the Slam Books."

"I can see that you are off to a good start. But Slam Books aren't too nice for anybody," says Mrs. Freeland.

"We don't write bad things about people in Slam Books, Mrs. Freeland," argues Margaret. "If we can't say something good about somebody, we just write 'Nice' or 'Sweet.' That's not being mean."

"Well, what are the good things to say?" asks Mrs. Freeland.

"Oh, you know, like *popular, adorable, tons of fun, cutest clothes, really pretty, the smartest one.* Things like that," Margaret rattles off.

"So 'nice' and 'sweet' are not such nice or sweet words? Or as a famous person once said, 'Damned by faint praise.' I hope I don't see any Slam Books this year. Now, let's get on with Geography. Renee, you are always up-to-date on France. Lead us off."

Renee rises. She is wearing a bra. I can see the straps through her blouse. "In occupied France, the sabotage to railroads is so bad that a reward of $20,000.00 (that's about a million francs) has been offered to anyone who would squeal on the saboteurs. We knew that the French were not taking the occupation lying down, but the Germans had tried to hush it up."

"Renee, I know you are proud of your countrymen. Can you tell the class what 'sabotage' means?"

"Oh, yes. 'Sabotage' is deliberate damage. It comes from the French word 'sabot,' which means 'wooden shoe.' Years ago, some workers threw their wooden shoes into factory machinery to mess it up and hurt production because they weren't being paid enough. Also, Mrs. Freeland there have been assassinations of Germans."

"Thank you, Renee. I hope your uncle is still safe."

"Yes, Mrs. Freeland. As far as we know."

"Who volunteers with Russian news?"

Becky Sue's hand goes up. She rises. Gosh, she's brave to volunteer the first day. I bet she'll be a leader. I wonder if she's smarter than Suzanna and I. She's wearing a cute skirt and I can see her bra straps too.

"President Roosevelt said that the Russians have an army of 15 million men. And that they are killing German soldiers and destroying tons of German weapons."

"Thank you, Becky Sue. Do you know what the Russians want from us?"

"I think so. They would like lend-lease like what we have given England, but our country is not going to do that. Russia will have to pay for everything, but it will be on easy terms. They want short range bombers, pursuit planes, tanks and anti-tank guns."

There are murmurs of admiration. What a beginning! She'll have a lot to live up to.

"It is staggering in numbers to think of 15 million men, isn't it, class? Does anyone know how many servicemen we have now?" Mrs. Freeland's eyes scan the room. Becky Sue's hand goes up, "Yes, ma'am. 1,700,000."

There are groans from the class.

"Sally, I bet you have some local news?"

Sally rises. "Yes, Mrs. Freeland. The zoo is now open only to Negroes on Tuesdays. They have been coming on Tuesdays, but white people have too. Now white people are not allowed on Tuesdays. The other six days are exclusively for whites, except for nurses with white children."

"Do you have any comment to make about that new ordinance?"

"Only that it seems Thursday would have been a better day because most cooks and nurses are off on Thursdays and of course, a half day on Sunday.

"Thank you, Sally. Just a brief Press summary for you before class is dismissed:

"The war of three continents has raged for two full years, but of the 731 days of conflict, only 528 have been spent in actual battle on land. The war in the air and on the sea has gone on continuously.

World War I was fought almost entirely in the trenches and at sea. Thus, the most staggering loses then were the lives of young men. With so much bombing of cities in this war, a cross section of population is being killed. Old men and women and children. About 60 civilians to one soldier."

"Maybe this year we will see peace, Mrs. Freeland," yearns Audrey.

"My daddy says that Colonel Lindbergh has the right idea. Not to get involved. That Hitler will win anyway. Daddy thinks we should put America first," offers Lulu timidly.

"A good beginning, my dears and my darlings. See you Monday," and Mrs. Freeland leaves the room.

"Dancing class starts this Saturday night," I say to Sally. We both look for Becky Sue, who is talking with Shirley and packing up her books.

"Would you like to go to Miss Adelaide's ballroom dancing class this Saturday night?" invites Sally. "You can go as our guest the first time."

"And my momma will call your mother and tell her about it," I add. "It's lots of fun."

"It is lots of fun, but Eliza can really say that because she is the Belle of the Ball," Sally continues. "The parents take turns driving."

"Thank you both. It does sound like fun and I'll talk to Mother when she gets home from work."

Chapter LX

THE NEW GIRL AT DANCING SCHOOL

"**G**ood evening, Miss Adelaide, I am Eliza and this is Sally 's and my guest, Becky Sue Smith."

"Good evening, Eliza and Sally. How lovely to see you again. And Becky Sue, welcome. Is 'Becky' a diminutive for 'Rebecca'?"

"No, Miss Adelaide," and Becky Sue makes a perfect half-curtsey.

"'Becky Sue' is the name by which you were christened?" Miss Adelaide asks gently.

"I wasn't christened, Miss Adelaide," and Becky Sue makes another perfect half-curtsey.

Sally and I exchange a quick look. Not christened?

"Well, welcome, Becky Sue. It is a pleasure to see your lovely manners," and Miss Adelaide looks to the next in line.

I love my new dress. It is dubonnet taffeta with silver buttons all the way down the front. It is cut on the princess line and goes in at the waist and goes out to make a wider skirt. My hair ribbons are pale aqua moire and so are my socks. I wish I had stockings, but Momma said I had to be 13 to have stockings. Becky Sue has on stockings! I didn't notice when she got in the car.

"Becky Sue, are you 13?"

"No, not 'til Christmas. Are you?"

"No, my birthday is in the summer. So is Sally's. How did your

Momma let you have stockings?"

"It's not all that long until Christmas and this is a special occasion. Do they look all right?"

"They look wonderful! They are not sagging around your ankles the way they do sometimes. Are they rayon? How do they feel?" I say, stupefied with wonder and jealousy.

"They aren't rayon. They are silk. And they feel super. Are my seams straight?" and Becky Sue turns around for us to check.

Her dress is pink and blue plaid and it goes in at the waist and it twirls as she turns around. Her blonde hair is tied up high in two pony tails--with pink and blue plaid bow ribbons. She smiles brilliantly. "Am I all right?" she asks anxiously.

"Yes, you are fine. And your seams are straight. Where did you get silk stockings? They are so expensive." I have got to know.

"My father sent them to me," Becky Sue answers, "from Chicago."

The music starts and we take our places on the benches. More boys than girls. Thank goodness! Nobody will be a wallflower. I see Hugh and Tommy and ... oh, here the boys come to ask for a dance. There is a rush across the room. They are rushing to Becky Sue! Even Tommy!

"Now, gentlemen, Becky Sue, can only dance with one at a time. Chose another partner quickly or you will dance with the broom," manages Miss Adelaide.

My face is red and my mouth is dry. The guys didn't rush to ask me to dance. What is wrong? Did everybody see?

"Oh, hey, Tommy. Yes, I would love to dance. Tell me about your summer," and we fox-trot like crazy.

"You are a great dancer, Eliza. Who is the new girl?"

"There are several new girls," I say, "Which one do you mean?"

Chapter LXI

THE NEW DRIVER

"Bill, will you drive Sally and me to the ten cent store to get cardboard for our geography project?"

"What's the matter with your feet?"

"Nothing is the matter with our feet. The boards are too large to carry. I thought with your new driver's license you would jump at the chance."

"O.K., but don't you two take all day."

"Sally, what is your project?"

"I'm going to put sand on mine and a few main cities and the battle lines for the desert war. You know, in North Africa. There was a great article in *Life* with pictures, a story and maps. I'm using the same title 'The Desert is Hell,'" Sally explains. "I'll paint a thermometer to show how hot is gets. The sun beats down so hard that the British soldier prefers to wear his pith helmet even in battle and to take the chance of a machine gun bullet through the head, rather than to roast his head under a steel helmet. Can you imagine?"

"No, I can't imagine the desert. I bet the sand is always in your mouth. Did the article say anything about mirages? I've always wondered if they were real."

"The article did say that mirages appear out of the shimmering heat."

"Scorpions are in the desert, too," adds Bill. "Do you still like bugs, sister-dear?"

"Oh, hush, I'm not afraid," I retort.

"Scorpions sting the men and cause arms and legs to swell three or four times their size."

"Well, I'm not in the desert and I'm not going. And my project is about Russia. And I'm using a *Life* magazine article, too. I'm calling my project 'Mud and Blood in Russia'. I'll make snow and mud and blood. I need to find some tiny toy soldiers at the store. Maybe I can find some that are wounded. Stalin claims he is stalling the Germans and that Nazi casualties are four and a half million!"

"I wonder what Suzanna's will be? And Becky Sue's? We know Renee's will be about France. And Audrey told me her project is about the part British women play in the war effort."

"Let's call and see if we can go over to Catherine's and work together. The sixth grade has the same assignment," I say. "And maybe we should call Margaret and she if she wants to come," I add.

"How are you going to get there or do I just assume that I am to be your private chauffeur?" Bill grins.

"Thank you. When does Momma want her car back?"

"Mrs. Long took her to bridge this afternoon, so I'm home free."

"Kress's had everything and I even took my change in defense stamps. Did you get everything, Sally?"

"I did and I did, too," comes Sally's muffled voice from behind the sand sacks.

"Thanks, brother-dear. Can you come back before dinner?"

"You be ready by five. I've got a big date," Bill lets the cat out of the bag.

"I bet it's with Connie, right?"

"Yep. We're going to see *A Yank in the R.A.F.*"

"With Betty Grable and Tyrone Power? Poppa loves Betty Grable."

"She's not bad. The really interesting thing is that the aerial battles in the movie are authentic and were filmed over Germany, France and England, with the full cooperation of the British Air Ministry. In other words, the Battle of Dunkirk and Betty Grable are sensational!" and Bill drives off.

"Hello, Mrs. Muzzy-dear. Catherine and Audrey are expecting us."

"Good afternoon, Eliza. Good afternoon, Sally. Please come in. The girls are in the sewing room with goodness-knows-what spread all around. Will you join us for tea at four?"

"Yes, Mrs. Muzzy-dear, thank you."

"Let me show you," says Catherine. "You know I'm interested in the Far East, China and Japan. There are eyewitness and pictorial evidence that Japan has used poison gas against China. Isn't that ghastly?"

"As you know, mine is about 'British Women in the War'. Mrs. Hunt let me cut these pictures out of an August *Life*. There are a million women in the WRENS, the Women's Royal Navy Service, and the WVS, Women's Voluntary Service. Another million are in factories, on farms, bus conductors, porters, railway workers, window cleaners, firefighters, butchers, blacksmiths. Mother says there is no time for tears," and Audrey shows us the pictures.

"Let's call Becky Sue and see what hers is," I suggest.

Becky Sue comes to the phone. "Hey, whatcha doing? My project? I'm doing one about the FBI: how it is smashing sabotage plots. Oh? Well, one example is just a simple sheet of music which the average person wouldn't be the least suspicious of. But an FBI agent examined it carefully and found that a spy had written a message with musical notes!"

"Wow! I guess everybody and everything is under suspicion.

That sounds really interesting. See you at dancing school tonight," I say.

"Are you going to the drug store afterward?" asks Becky Sue.

"No," I say. My heart pounds. I wonder if Tommy asked her. "Are you?"

"No. Nobody has asked me, but I hear that people go sometimes."

I breathe a quiet sigh of relief.

Chapter LXII

FRIDAY NIGHT PARTY WITH BOYS

"Sally, have you talked to Helen?

"Yes. She just called."

"What did your mother say? Can you go?"

"She said she would talk with your mother."

"Momma's not home yet. I'll have her call your mother. Do you want to go?"

"I guess so. Yes, I do want to go. I would hate not to be invited," confides Sally.

"Is Helen having the whole class?"

"I bet she is. I wonder where she is getting the boys."

"From dancing class, from her Sunday School, from her friends last year at Miss Lee's. Does she have a brother? Maybe some of his friends, if he is the right age. I wonder if she will invite Drew," I giggle at the last.

"What kind of party is it? What will we do?"

"She says it is an Open House. She'll have records to play and cokes and potato chips and toll house cookies. Her daddy is going to roll up the rug in the living room," I am talking and thinking at the same time. How will we manage without Miss Adelaide to run things. "Oh, here is Momma now. Bye."

Helen's house is ablaze with lights and Glenn Miller music. And lots of high-pitched laughter and squeals. We all decided to wear saddle oxford shoes and skirts and sweaters. Mine are the plain ones from Derrick's; for Christmas, I want a pair of Spaldings like Suzanna's and Becky Sue's. I like my blue sweater. it is a deep, real blue that makes my blue eyes bigger and bluer. And I like my plaid skirt. It has box pleats in the front, back, and on the side, so it really twirls right.

It looks as though the whole class is here. I don't know all the boys. But there is Drew! I'll pretend I don't see him for a moment until I can think of something to say. "Oh, hey, Tommy, how are you? Isn't this super?"

"Hey, Eliza. Is this your whole class? There are new guys and girls in my class too."

"Aren't you at Belleview Junior High now? I'd be so glad to be rid of that Miss Wells. How is your new principal?"

"So far, so good. Mr. Roper. But he doesn't take any nonsense off of anybody. He uses the paddle too, but not like Miss Wells, just to be mean. Would you like to go to the drug store tomorrow night?"

"I would love to, Tommy. Thank you. I have to check with Momma to be sure though."

"I know. I'll call you tomorrow. Hugh is asking Sally. And Roy is calling Becky Sue. She surely is a cute girl."

"She is a cute girl and she's smart, too," I say with my brightest smile. "I wonder if anybody is going to dance without a broom to threaten them," I smile some more at Tommy.

"Do you want to dance?"

"Sure. You are a great dancer, Tommy," and I smile again. My jaws hurt. This must be what Miss Adelaide means about acting like you are having a good time.

"Can I break in on you, Tom, ole boy?" Drew is tapping Tommy on the shoulder.

"Sure, Drew. See you, Eliza."

"Thank you, Tommy," and I smile at him. Then, I turn to Drew. "Hey, Drew. It's so nice to see you." I make my voice lilt.

"Thanks. How's my stand-in-princess? You must be great because you look like you're having such a good time."

I flip my head back and laugh a little. "Oh, Drew. How are you? Are you in a new school this year? Tell me about it." and I smile some more. My jaws are cracking.

"No, same school, but I'm on the basketball team this year."

"Oh you are? Really? That is super! I know boys' basketball is harder than girls'. When do you play?"

"We practice four afternoons a week and we always have at least one game. Why? Do you want to come?"

"Oh, Drew, I would love to come. You just tell me when and where and Sally and I will both come, both of your princesses. My brother is driving now and I know he would bring us." I smile some more. My jaws are killing me. "I am so thirsty. Do you want to get a coke?"

"Sure, let's do. And Mrs. Evans makes the best cookies." Drew hands me a coke and we both get chips and cookies and move over to Sally and Hugh.

"Hello, first princess," greets Drew. "It looks like your leg is all well."

"Hey, prince. Thanks. The only thing is I can't go up on my right toes. But I'm not a toe dancer anyway. I leave that to Eliza," Sally smiles and laughs.

"Are you riding with your dad?"

"Oh, yes. But I'm not jumping yet. What are you doing?"

"Playing basketball. Eliza said you and she would come to see your prince on the court. That would be great to have my own rooting team."

Drew is so absolutely cool that I could just absolutely scream. I just smile some more and say, "Isn't this the most super party?"

There is no music. Someone has not put on a new record. Someone has dimmed the lights. Everybody is making a big circle. What is going on? Someone puts on "Dancing in the Dark." Everybody starts to sit on the floor in the circle. The boys are pushing and shoving each other. Someone says, "Tommy, you're IT!" and a coke bottle is twirled in the middle of the circle.

It stops and points to Becky Sue. "O.K., Tommy, kiss Becky Sue!"

Everybody laughs louder and claps. We are playing 'Spin the Bottle'! I've heard about it, but I never thought about it and I don't have time to think about it now. I'm in it! Tommy is giving Becky Sue a peck on the cheek.

"That's not good enough, Tommy. Kiss her on the mouth." More clapping and laughter.

I can't look, but I want to. Is Becky Sue embarrassed? I've never kissed anybody. I don't know how. I wonder if she knows how. I've got to look and see if she closes her eyes.

Tommy says, "O.K.. Come here, Becky Sue," and he kisses her on the mouth! Not for long though. But he kissed her! She closed her eyes.

"O.K., Tommy, you can choose someone to be IT."

"I choose Hugh. Your turn, fella," and Tommy gives the coke bottle a fierce turn. Everybody squeals as it turns. It stops and points at a space between me and Sally.

"Spin again," I say quickly. "It didn't land on anybody."

"Oh, shucks. I thought I would get to kiss you both," cracks Hugh. The guys are really getting into the spirit of this. And Tommy gives the bottle another spin. I hold my breath. It lands on Sally!

"Come here, Sally. This is the chance of your lifetime," says

Hugh and gives her a quick gentle kiss on the mouth. I hope Sally is not embarrassed. She closed her eyes.

"O.K. I choose Drew to be IT!" and Hugh gives the bottle a lazy spin. It wobbles around and lands on ME! I hear people shouting my name, but I'm not sure I can stand up. Sally gives me a hand and I hear Drew saying, "O.K., stand-in-princess, we've got another performance to do," and he kisses me firmly on the mouth and squeezes my hand and everybody shouts, "That's a good one, Drew!"

I think I'm going to faint!

Chapter LXII

A NEW CHAPTER IN ELIZA'S LIFE

I've been kissed! I've been kissed! Drew kissed me! Even if it was only a 'Spin the Bottle' game." Is that naughty? Is it wrong to play 'Spin the Bottle'? I didn't know we were going to. Is that what happens at all-boy and girl parties? Who started it? Where were Helen's parents? What if they had walked in? Would they have sent us all home in disgrace? I wonder if anybody on the bus can tell by looking at me that I have been kissed?

I pull the cord for the stop in front of Gerber's and hurry to the Tea Room to meet Sally and Suzanna. We order cream cheese sandwiches on raisin toast and cokes. We look at each other and break out laughing.

"I guess the joke is on us!"

"Suzanna, who kissed you?"

"Mark. I've known him all my life. I just never thought I would ever kiss him. I wonder if he will tell. Eliza, how was it to kiss Drew?"

"I don't really know. I was so scared. But he said something sweet and he squeezed my hand. There is something to older boys."

"Sally, tell us about Hugh."

"Well, Hugh is fine and he is such a dear old friend that I wasn't embarrassed. It wasn't like having to kiss a stranger."

"Will we have that game every time we have a boy-girl party

without Miss Adelaide?" wonders Suzanna.

"I don't think so. My parents would be around all the time," Sally says.

"Mine, too," I echo, "or my brother."

"Will those guys think we are fast? Will they talk about us?"

"They're probably talking just the way we are now," Sally laughs and then looks at the clock on the Tea Room wall. "Time for the movie. Aren't we going to Loew's Palace?"

"I can't wait to see John Wayne and Sonja Henie. I'm sure they'll kiss. I'm going to watch closer to see how they do it," I announce.

"And Glenn Miller's orchestra plays. It's *Sun Valley Serenade*. It's very romantic."

"We need all the tips we can get," I laugh. The three of us lock arms and sing, "We're off to see the Wizard, the Wonderful Wizard of Oz!"

About the Author

Emily Boone Ruch was born in Memphis, TN, educated at Bruce and Miss Hutchison's schools. She majored in English at Duke University and graduated Phi Beta Kappa. She received a Masters Degree in US history and a secondary school teacher certificate from Memphis State University. She and her husband reared three children, four standard poodles, and two "rescues."